Fluffy Psychopaths

By Diana Armstrong

Diana Armstrong
dianaarmstrong@yahoo.com
Glasgow, Scotland

Acknowledgements

I dedicate this book to all the people who loved me at some point in their lives. Thank you for teaching me the necessary survival skills to not only heal – but to thrive and love life fervently. Together we kicked history's ass.

Preparation stage

In 1973 Anna-Ray attempted to kill her brother. The plan was badly conceived, poorly executed, and ultimately unsuccessful. But then again, she was only four at the time. Anna-Ray is now a loving mum.

Grant learned at 19 how to use a machete to kill silently in the jungle. He beheaded dozens of Japanese soldiers and collected their ears on his belt. His voice was silky smooth, his lips sensuous and his Elvis impressions better than the original.

Saskia, a bright woman and survivor of a Nazi children's camp, knowingly chose a sadistic violent paranoid schizophrenic paedophile as the babysitter for her little four year old girl, and, despite plenty of warning signs, did nothing to protect her. The ordeal lasted ten years and only ended when he was committed to a mental health facility. Not for what he had done to Saskia's daughter. He slapped

*his psychiatrist. Saskia still denies any of this ever
happened. All of her children love her deeply.*

*We all strive to survive not only what was done to us,
but worse, what we have done to others. Mere physical
survival is not enough, we need to live. We get better and
better at rewriting our past, we create constructs that reflect
who we would like to have been. Like Chinese whispers,
stories change the more often we tell them. After a while we
muddle up dates and places, we forget which version we
told whom. Narrative therapy, a great tool for moving on, at
the same time fragments us. How can we feel truly loved if
no one knows who we really are? Can we ever regain a
whole and integrated self? Is it possible to change those
constructs before the varnish sets?*

Session 1

Have you ever been in a trance before? Don't worry, you will not lose consciousness in this process, you can trust me. You will at all times be able to hear everything, and you will be able to attend to any crisis. At the end of this you will be able to remember everything. It will be as if you have been daydreaming, nothing more.

While you are taking all this in, I want you to notice your body relaxing. Let's count down from three to one and notice yourself sinking into a comfortable hypnotic trance. Three – your arms and limbs become heavy and relaxed, two – your neck and shoulders are soft and relaxed, one – your entire body is deeply relaxed, you breathe slowly and deeply, your heart beats slowly and in perfect rhythm, allowing you to let go completely.

I would like you now to imagine a set of stairs in front of you, ten steps going down. You decide to go down the steps one by one, and with each step you feel yourself drifting deeper. Ten, going deeper into relaxation. Nine, deeper still. Eight, you are beginning to feel the sensation of complete relaxation and trance. Seven, you enter an even deeper state of trance. Six, you are now completely focussed on entering an even deeper state of trance. Five, with each step and each breath you allow yourself to drift deeper and deeper. Four, you are almost there, that's right. Three, you are now in a very deep trance. Two, you begin to sense that your unconscious mind is almost ready to enter this journey. One, you are there, in a deep trance, ready to begin.

I want you now to imagine travelling in time and place. You are travelling to Hamburg, a modern and thriving metropolis in the North of Germany. It is the 29th of May, 1998. You feel yourself flying high above this city. You approach it from the North Sea in the west and follow the massive river Elbe, flying east, past white sandy beaches lining the river, with locals waving at passing ocean liners, until you arrive at the harbour. You can see cranes lifting countless containers off ships, each a different colour, and placing them gently onto their dedicated parking spot. You see the shipyards Blohm and Voss, with a huge ferry awkwardly propped up in its dry dock. You watch tourists strolling along the Reeperbahn, shocked and attracted in equal measure by the open display of nudity. Dildos in shop windows, so big you can make out their shape even from up here. Somewhere down there, in one of the old nightclubs, the concept of the Beatles was born. You smell the frying oil wafting up from the many food stalls selling Kartoffelpuffer mit Apfelmus – potato fritters with apple mash. You take a deep breath and then cough as your nostrils are assaulted by the stench of fish guts, left down there at the fish market after this morning's trade. From far away you make out a few notes of live Jazz music, bravely trying to hold their own amidst ferry horns calling out to their passengers, bicycle bells and traffic noise.

You decide to change direction and head North, below you the Alster, a massive lake in the heart of the city. A small part is split off from the rest by two parallel running bridges, creating a smaller lake right next to the main shopping street, the Jungfernstieg. Café and restaurant boats line this part of the lake, it smells of money. Further up, you see joggers running along the promenade, chased by obesity and heart failure. The water is lined with cherry trees, all in full blossom right now. You drift a little to your right and follow a dual carriageway; the scene is becoming a little greyer now, asphalt lined thinly by trees and shrubs, dotted with traffic lights. A building in front of you now, a large glass front, with offices on the ground floor and flats above the third. It is the top flat we are interested in, on the fifth floor. You are high enough to peek into the window and can make out a large living room, wooden floor, covered with carpets, a children's climbing frame on the back wall. You are pleased to discover you can glide through the window pane and fly closer to the bathroom door, which is locked. No barrier for you, you find yourself inside and catch your first glimpse of Anna-Ray, lying in the bath. She is almost twenty-nine at this stage.

You can feel the bath water, which has long grown cold. The young woman slides deeper, too weak to hold herself upright, until her knees emerge and her lips touch the water line, leaving a metallic taste in her mouth. Her breasts are floating; her nipples stand erect just above the surface. He would love to see me like this, you hear her think, and her nausea overwhelms you a little. What would it be like to vomit into a bathtub? Another fluid added to the cauldron. She is already enveloped in clouds of blood, mixed with sperm, would it matter? Anna-Ray was raised near the sea. A true water baby, even her star sign is cancer. Accustomed to the wide open spaces of North Germany, the amaranthine beach of Travemünde - with its whirlpools of soft sand torn back and forth by lunar gravity - she too had found herself pulled into marriage and torn away from it. A single mum now, she had found this birds' nest made of glass, perched on top of a tall office building, the ideal place to raise her child and herself. Other women in the same position had to make do with life in one of the small walk in toilets with bed settee that were fully funded by the benefits office. In this huge, stunningly beautiful and unforgivingly expensive city, Anna-Ray had researched and researched until she had found this oasis. She had recognised immediately that this rather ugly and industrial street was too close to the city centre to appeal to families and too big and homely to appeal to business tenants. With her journalist connections she had soon found out how long the place had been standing empty. Using her feminine guiles and ignoring her feminist guilt she had flirted the landlord into submission, when he, glad to have found anyone to contribute to his monthly mortgage, had finally given in with a deep sigh and had rented her the flat for a third of its market value. Maybe her semi iconic status as the voice of the Hamburg underground trains had helped. "Nächste Haltestelle Berliner Tor" – next stop, Berliner Tor. It had been her voice that carried her and her child from electricity bill to rent check. She recorded news items, political documentaries, answer phone messages. Even mild erotica, when money was tight. Her full sensuous lips managed to produce that velvet tone that seduces listeners to stay glued to the radio, while taking in none of the content. And again, the little feminist whisper that told her she had to earn her living, not just profit from her sex appeal, was muffled under a pile of household bills.

Was this payback? Why had she opened the door? Why had she not fought back? She lived in a high security flat, her door was fire proof, and yet she had opened it, merely because her uninvited visitor had been holding a bunch of flowers. The last in a long line of self proclaimed lovers, an experiment gone too far, fantasy becoming torn flesh. Undoubtedly, her life had led her to this moment. It made perfect sense. When she lost her husband to a separate bedroom, then a separate house, she had begun to test herself. He took their child half of the week. Days, when she decided to meet pain head on. She wanted to push herself. Hard. Maybe that would dislodge that sticky knot in her chest. The internet was a new thing, but she had never shied away from technology. The possibility to live out fantasies purely in cyberspace had been too delicious to resist, so she joined a chat room for S&M fans. It had still been frustrating to write a line, which responded to something another participant had typed three thoughts ago. The fantasy had been destroyed by the disjointedness of the narrative and any arousal disintegrated. Finally, today's visitor had invited her into a private chat room. Step by step, her inhibitions had fallen away and they had both crossed the threshold into disturbia, verbalising a world in which victims love to be tortured, orifices are to be explored with tools and knives as well as giant cocks, whether attached to a man or operated by batteries. When she finally reached her limit and decided to log off, he sent her messages urging to meet in person. Imagination was one thing, reality was rather more unforgiving, it came with permanent scars, prison sentences and therapist bills. She did not want to cross that disinhibition threshold. But she was in the public eye and had made the mistake of telling him about her claim to fame – when he had asked for her phone number she had told him facetiously that he could hear her whenever he liked as the voice announcing stations on the Hamburg underground. He had researched her, and had found her photo on the website of the radio station where she occasionally read the news. From there to following her home it must have been only a small step. If she reported this, the papers would have a field day. She was in the middle of a custody battle with her ex husband; she could not take any risks. She could not stay here either. The rapist had her address now. Her child's address.

All her life she had believed that, once she was a grown woman, she would rip anyone apart who tried to harm her, and yet, when this game went too far her fighting spirit had congealed in her veins. Like a deer staring at the headlights she had obeyed his every wish, had separated from her body and floated up to the ceiling, watching him split her lips, crush her cheekbones, shatter her teeth, the shards digging into her cheeks from the inside. The child had been asleep in his bedroom; she had not made a sound, not a whimper. When he had left, she had stuffed a kitchen towel between her legs, wiped the blood off the floor, picked up the torn flowers and disposed of them.

You take in the moment as you look at her now with complete mindfulness. There is a strange beauty about the way in which the red sap haemorrhages in waves and swirls, forming clouds in the bath water before spreading out into a light pink, absorbed into the miniature ocean. Too shallow to drown her, deep enough to dilute the evidence. Were the little sperm tadpoles still alive? Hundreds, maybe millions of potential half humans swimming around her broken body like piranhas, stripping her flesh, exposing the structure underneath. But there are her own blood cells, too, just as alive, just as potent – you spur them on, imagine them waging a war. In a small shelf beside the bath tub you spot a well worn copy of Patrick Süskind's *Das Parfüm*. Above the shelf a family crest. One muscular arm, raised to strike, fist clenched. *Invictus maneo*, you read, I remain unvanquished. You can see the beginnings of a bruise covering the left side of her face, which has already swollen beyond recognition. Her smile would be different now. A few teeth missing. You share your own instinctive response with her. You float a little closer and whisper into her brain "Leave!" And then you do.

Session Two

Jump with me. Jump way back, into the past, a small mining village in County Durham, Britain. It is the 24th July 1925. A small row of cottages, built especially for the miners and their families. I know, it is difficult to imagine this scene without resorting to clichés learned in films and books. And, in a way, we are here to observe a typical scene. The man of the house, John is still away, he followed in his father's, brothers' and uncle's dusty footsteps, followed them deep into the mine shaft, into an honest day's work, into a man's well deserved pride for being a good provider, into chronic pulmonary disease and broken backs. From the age of thirteen, the men were trying to find carbonized organic matter. And they found the black beauty, tons of it, by candlelight, snuggled up to collier's lung, black spittle, miners' anaemia, miners' elbow and stinkdamp – at least they would never be alone down there.

But here, in this house, another member of the village is fulfilling her duty. As a wife, Thomasina has to produce enough offspring to ensure a pension for John and herself. Her face, not beautiful by common standards, is drenched in sweat, distorted by pain. Every muscle is tense, neck and shoulders have turned to stone, her legs want to kick not spread, how can anything be pressed out of this woman's body? Even her wails have to work their way out, from the depth of her gut through gritted teeth.

Can you smell the coal fire? Can you smell the copper kettle, the scrubbed stone tiles, the damp? Come on, you can do better than this, put your back into it. Throw in a few words of Geordie, it will make it feel much more real.

'Come on, hinny, any time now. I can see the head. We want to present John with a strong little bairn when he comes home, don't we?' The midwife is trying to sound encouraging. She could see the head two hours ago. It's stuck. This one wants to see the skies, not look down onto bloodied sheets like the others. Back to back labour. Proud little thing. Inconsiderate little bugger. Get out, get out, you're butchering your mum. Another contraction ruptures

Thomasina's spine, voices are muffled now, lights become brighter.

John can't hear the screams but he can feel them, in the nape of his neck, in those little hairs that send shivers down his spine. The same hairs that stand up when his wife steps behind him, kisses his shoulders and lets her tongue run down his back. He draws breath. It's warm today, one of those gentle breezes that make you want to run away, jump on a train to Whitley Bay. Smell the salt in the air, mixed with the cinnamon scent of sunburned skin. She must have had the child by now, she started yesterday morning. Not even her first had been this stubborn. He strides along Dipton road, a handsome man, tall, would be taller still if his back had not been bent by the mines. He is wearing hoggers, the miner's shorts, and a simple flannel shirt that may have been white once but, despite persistent scrubbing, blends in now with the grey of his skin. He picks up pace, heavy boots on cobble. On the steps of his end of terrace sits Mary, his gentle six year old. Knees tucked under her chin she wraps herself around her doll. 'Is it over, Mary?' 'I don't know. Mummy screamed so much, Miss Turner called the doctor. But she stopped now.' It's a good thing she can't see how the blood drains from her father's face under a thick layer of coal dust. 'Has Dr Wigham been long?' No answer, a brief shrug of the shoulders.

There's clarts on yer boots, man. She doesn't have to be here, he can hear his wife's voice in his head. John steps out of his heavy work shoes and places them inside, next to the entrance on a sheet of newspaper, joined by his Davy lamp, his baccy box and empty tin flask. He shakes off the dust from his clothes and steps into the narrow corridor. Today there won't be the usual zinc tub waiting for him in the kitchen. No pot pie boiling, wrapped in cloth. No singing hinnie for afters. Instead of his tea there's water boiling on the stove. Fresh linen is drying on the pulley. All is prepared for the new life. For a brief moment he realises that this might now be his job. How would he raise a baby on his own, Mary is too young to help, his own father blind from the coal. He mustn't ruminate. His mother sneaks her way into his head, Mary Jane, gave birth to twenty four but only life to six. His last daughter Marian was taken from them after six weeks. Nine months pregnancy, twelve hours of labour, forty-two sleepless nights and one morning waking up to silence. If this is how it's going to be he doesn't want to know. Not now. But he reminds himself he has Jack, his oldest, he has Tiny and Mary, all of them well, knock on wood. He falls into the big chair before the fire, the same in which Thomasina spent every free minute of the last month sewing, and listens.

The fire is dying down. John rises from the chair, adds some coal. Time to organise something to eat, Mary will be hungry. There should still be some bread, he knows Thomasina baked on Monday. The silence upstairs has sucked the marrow from his bones. He has trouble standing upright. Finally. Dr Wigham steps into the kitchen. He is a small man, thin and bony. His moustache is kept immaculately clean, his cheeks, normally yellowish pale, are flushed with excitement. John can feel the news before he hears it. 'Congratulations, Mr Armstrong, it's a boy. Reluctant little bugger but strong and healthy nevertheless.' When John doesn't answer he continues: 'Miss Turner fetched me on time. Don't be surprised, the wee one has quite a dent, I had to use the forceps.' Only now does John become aware that his shoulders have been drawn up to his earlobes. With a sigh he drops them and heads towards the stairs. The doctor glances at his dirty work clothes and holds him back. 'Give them a bit of rest now, they have earned it. Maybe you should take a bath and then go up, what do you think?' John nods. 'Your wife has worried us a little, that much I can tell you. I think she is through the worst just now, but make sure you take her to the infirmary within the next few days for an operation. Then we'll see.'

Infirmary, operation, you have a son, forceps, take a bath. This is too much information to take in all at once. Take a bath, find food for Mary. Breathe. Thomasina is ok. The two men exchange nods, knowing very well that the Armstrongs have neither the time nor the money for an operation. When the midwife comes down, John takes a tin out from behind the bread bin. They have saved up for the fee.

Mary experiences the birth of her brother in her own way. She is staring at a curled up cabbage leaf that someone must have dropped from the garbage. A caterpillar emerges from its insides, as thick as her middle finger. Maybe it wants to warm up in the evening sun. She strokes the furry green skin and lets it crawl over the back of her hand. Right this moment the doctor and midwife leave the house. She knows the birth is over, everything is well. From this day Mary will believe that babies are brought by caterpillars. You know, because she told you when you two were waiting together on the steps. You did not correct her.

The arrival of the new Armstrong is reason enough to celebrate in the King's Arms. What is his name going to be? Joseph, after the old Armstrong or Matthew, after Thomasina's dad? John does not find the courage to offend either of them. A few pints of stout later he informs the crowd – the Durham chapel of Dipton will welcome a new sheep into their midst, a sheep called Grant.

Session Three

Let's give you a break, we will only take a short trip this time, a tiny step north, to the airport in Newcastle. Let's make it easy on you and return to modern day, let's not put a date on it, let's call it NOW.

We will head for the arrivals gate; we need to meet a few guys there. Their plane landed twenty minutes ago, but you know how it is, even with a fanfare of *yet another plane arrived on time*, it takes a while before the fasten seatbelt sign has been switched off, the steps connected to the plane, doors have opened and passengers have retrieved their suitcases from lockers nowhere near their seat. Security checks, passport control. Pleasure or business, sir? Neither, really. No goods to declare, a Starbucks, a bookshop, a couple of car hire counters. This could have been anywhere. Nine men in dark clothing, one by one, approach the car hire desks. Each picks up one car, as if unaware they are headed in the same direction, here for the same purpose. What a waste of fuel, I agree. They need to believe they are unique.

In procession, they drive west along Hadrian's Wall. One driver in particular is clearly unaccustomed to driving on the left side of the road, causing a number of near miss incidents at roundabouts. They meet with the A7 and we follow them up north. Shortly after the sign Welcome to Scotland – Céad Míle Fáilte – they are abruptly halted by a small traffic light. At amber, the cars move across a narrow stone bridge, past a blackened metal sculpture of riders, an artistic distraction from tenement buildings, concrete towers overlooking Brigadoon. A cloud of sickening sweetness envelopes this place. On closer inspection you discover its source – the tannery, where workers scrape intestines and other flesh off sheeps' skins, transforming them into cozy carpets and luxury gloves. Welcome to Langholm, the Muckle Toon, mocks the sign, advertising the grey town, solid and fortified, nestled into a soft green valley in the Borders. Birthplace of Hugh McDiarmid, it boasts, omitting the fact that the Scottish poet and politician, while born here as Christopher Murray Grieve, couldn't wait to change his name and move away. The narrow main street leads the cars past shops: a Costcutters, a pharmacy, a post office, a Chinese takeaway, most of them closed. A small corner cafe advertises homemade ice cream, a small child ties his shoelaces, he doesn't look up. There is not much interest in the outside world. 'A day outside Langholm is a wasted day' is the motto of this town. At the Telford Bridge they turned left, following the signs towards Samye Ling, the not so distant Tibetan Buddhist temple, then left again at the old primary school. Opposite an ancient graveyard they turn right, up a steep path, hesitating whether the instructions could possibly have been correct. The small cars are built for economy, not mountaineering, and some of the engines struggle to catch their breath, climbing further and further, past the gamekeeper's cottage, past the farm, through a gate, negotiating a few lazy sheep on the path, until, quite unexpectedly, they arrive at the top, their composure lost in the view. They switch off their engines and park on the grass, just in front of Upper Caulfield, an old cottage on the lands of the Duke of Buccleuch.

There was a time when the boundaries between Scotland and England were blurred. Both sides claimed the land between Carlisle and Langholm, so the forty square miles of twilight zone remained known as the Debateable Lands for over three hundred years.

The Armstrongs were one of the dominant clans here. It is said that at one time they could assemble as many as 3000 horsemen, frequently venturing outside the boundaries, marked by the rivers Liddel, Esk and Sark, raiding farms and homesteads. They never wore the kilt - any man who has ever had the discomfort of sharp edged horsehair digging into his unprotected groin will sympathise - they chose the trews, trousers made from the tartan cloth of their clan. Reivers had no king, no country; they rode the Middle Marches unhindered by law or morality. The outcry 'Are there no Christians among you – No, we are Armstrongs and Elliotts' became as famous as Logan Mack's translation of the 1551 proclamation of the Crown officers: "All Englishmen and Scottishmen, after this proclamation made, are and shall be free to rob, burn, spoil, slay, murder and destroy all and every such persons, their bodies, buildings, goods and cattle as do remain or shall inhabit upon any part of the said Debatable Land without any redress to be made for the same."

When a reiver's wife noticed the larder was empty, she served up a pair of spurs instead of dinner, a hint it was time to go 'shopping' in the neighbourhood.

How much blood had nursed the soil of the Borders, from the ancient battles to the Lockerbie crash? Anna-Ray had read once that a Hungarian countess used to bathe in the blood of virgins to preserve her beauty. Maybe there was something to this idea – the gentle curves of these hills, enveloped in soft grass, caressed by impatient shadows of clouds, had preserved their timeless allure.

When the men leave their cars, they stand still, contemplating the setting. After all, they have been summoned to attend a funeral, the occasion demands a little solemnity. From this hill they can see the land stretch out as far as the Solway Firth, they listen to the squawking of seagulls and taste fresh green in the air.

One could hide in a place like this, one could sledge with a child in the moonlight, sit on the grass, arms wrapped around knees, examine scars and think. One could rest here and hope that the soil was finally saturated.

Anna-Ray had made all arrangements herself. She had pre-ordered the ceremony, the type of music she wanted, the place where the willow coffin was to be buried – and, although eternally broke, had paid for it in advance. This should have been surprising, considering how suddenly she was silenced in the end, but this one had never left much to chance. A final joke on the men in her life – it seemed she had invited every single one of them. The solicitor had had trouble carrying out her will and had needed to hire a private investigator to track them all down, a task made all the harder by the fact that she had lived in Germany most of her sexually active life. And here they were, the fruit of his labour and her pleasure. A group of men, confused, some sad, some angry at the sight of the others, together at the top of a hill. She had come here often, every autumn, to attend the Clan Armstrong gather, and had fallen in love with the place. She had always said she might move here one day, give her son a proper childhood, hide away avocados in nests of grass, pretending they were dragons' eggs (Yes, thank you for pointing out that she learned this from a Billy Connolly routine. You are quite right but stay with me here). She hid fairy letters in the cracks of a tree trunk for the astonished boy to find, along with little presents of chocolates. (Yes, the chocolates were part of a series of miniature chocolates, called *Garden Fairies* produced by the chain of shops selling mock Victorian tat, called "Past Times", stop spoiling the atmosphere and take a deep breath. Relax. Now come back.) She told the child old stories in front of an open fire, there may have even been chestnuts roasted but let's not push it.

Right now it is a cold day, stormy and wet, not unusual for this little corner of the universe. Walter, now 36, probably deserves the most credit for turning up. They all are busy, all have full schedules, if, however, lives that are slightly emptier now she is gone. He came in his wheelchair, accompanied by his nurse Sigmund, another male in the crowd of mourners that knew Anna-Ray intimately. She had left before Walter had been diagnosed with multiple sclerosis. Was it a small mercy or insulting to know it was him, not the disease that had chased her away? They had been friends at school, back in Germany, best buddies – so inseparable that she had granted him a ringside view when she hopscotched her way out of childhood, overstepping every single line she could find. Why had she called them to this godforsaken place in Scotland? Was she challenging them even now? Gauging their keenness, their residual love for her? Or was this one last joke? They had shared a warped sense of humour as school children, visiting specialist shops in the afternoon, asking for asparagus fittings at the iron monger's, and for click snort switches at the electrician's. It had been hard to keep a serious face while the assistants had frantically attempted to track down the elusive objects. Only once had they gone too far together, pouring sample packs of washing powder into the fountain in the city centre. No less than four fire engines had been necessary to suck away the foam. This kind of behaviour was unheard of. They both enjoyed the feeling of empowerment these little derelictions gave them. At eleven years old, Walter had been assigned as his grandfather's carer. His mother had done this job before, but she was now battling chemotherapy herself. Walter had no choice when it came to cleaning up faeces or directing the bedridden old man's penis into the opening of a urine bottle. Anna-Ray's cries for attention had been ignored since early childhood, so she enjoyed immensely the attention of passers by watching the clean up of the foam invasion. They had caused this. All this just because of them. Walter had been overweight in those days, but always keen to impress her. His favourite trick had been to pretend to jump onto pigeons, knowing well they would flutter away at the last second. Until, one day, one of the little birds had not moved out of the way on time. It had been messy.

They had grown up in a small town near Hanover, one of the few that had never been bombed in the war. As a consequence, all houses were perfectly preserved in their medieval styles, with wooden beams criss crossing through the facades. The houses had been taxed according to how much ground they covered, leading to one story stacked on top of another, expanding further and further outward with each added level like an upside down three tiered wedding cake, beautifully decorated with painted garlands of flowers and proud golden lettering – witness to status as well as the owner's god fearing lifestyle. The little town was so picture perfect, American tourists often asked where they were supposed to pay the entrance fee. Sometimes hornets, as thick and long as a man's thumb, would set up nest in the rotten beams, and rumours circulated that multiple bites by these little monsters could kill a grown person. But with both insects and buildings protected by law, there was not much one could do but draw a wide circle. Anna-Ray had learned quickly never to agitate a hornet, especially never to poke into the opening of the nest with a stick. She refused to believe the rumours of the fatal venom, but, having experienced the pain a mere wasp sting could generate, the thought of being invaded by such enormous stingers was enough to quell her curiosity.

Walter had often walked to school with her. She had been afraid of the British soldiers in front of the Naafi building, shouldering their semi-automatics. The war had ended 40 years before, long before she was born, but in the absence of a signed peace treaty Germany was still officially occupied. After fire-starting a war that had cost the lives of 50 million humans, the German military forces had unconditionally surrendered on May 8th, 1945. There had been no official peace until 1990, when the 2+4 treaty was signed by East and West Germany as well as the Soviet Union, Great Britain, the United States and France.

The allied forces had divided the country up like a pie. The Russians had sliced off the East and lined the edges with mines and armed guards. Berlin, trapped in the middle of the Eastern part, gave a caesarean birth to a massive wall, but the umbilical chord, linking West Berlin to West Germany by way of a closely guarded motorway, remained uncut.

French soldiers chose the Southern part of the country, leaving the Dutch, British and Americans to set up camp in the North. As a teenager, Anna-Ray had learned the difference easily, Americans behaved like gentlemen, calling you ma'am and holding open the door for you, Dutch behaved like best friends, with their long hair and relaxed attitude they were also the only ones who spoke German. The British Squaddies were the ones to watch. Dressed in T Shirt, Jeans and worn trainers no matter what the weather, they often sported self inflicted cigarette burns next to *I love my mum* tattoos on their forearms. Their quarrelsome behaviour and leaning to binge drinking had earned them numerous bans. In fact, most pubs displayed the sign 'Out of bounds' on their front entrance.

Walter was with Anna-Ray when she decided to sleep with her first boyfriend. He was there when she regretted it. He held her when she cried and laughed with her once she was over it. Like Steve McQueen's little rubber ball, she had joked, I bounce back faster the harder they throw me. When, much later, they finally began to sleep together, he was surprised how easy it was to fall for the illusion. He wanted her to stay and he wanted her to stay with him. For good. He knew of her past, he knew her demons and he was willing to protect her from them. So many men, none of them good enough for her. No wonder she kept running from them. Why shouldn't he be the one that got her to settle down? He showed her that he had kept all his drawings of her, since school days, big soft lips, dutifully curled up to a smile, soft brown eyes, like the eyes of a dead deer Walter's father shot not so long ago on a hunting trip. Remember the pigeon? She had replied and then she was gone. What good would this act do her now, he wondered. He was tired, what was he doing here?

It is now two thirty in the afternoon. The Scottish ground is too soggy for the wheelchair. Whatever they were expected to do, they would have to do it here. He has come this far with her and would go no further. He wondered what else she had planned for the day. Sigmund had sat down on the grass beside his chair. They had not addressed the fact that both had slept with her at one time of their lives. There was no need to talk about it. Sigmund had gone out with her when they were still at school. They had met in philosophy class, or values and norms, as it was called then. Anna-Ray had entrusted Walter with an intimate account of her relationship with Sigmund, blow by blow, as if to prove she was right about his being straight. He knew they had sneaked away camping together and he knew that in that tent Sigmund was the one to lose his virginity. Although he had never seen him naked, he knew he was covered in birthmarks and had the smooth skin of a girl. He hadn't changed at all. The same curly hair, the same John Lennon glasses. Years ahead of Beckham, he had surprised his class mates by wearing a sarong to school. Walter knew how impressed and intimidated Anna-Ray had been. She had fallen for the glasses and name, believing them to be proof of his superior intellect. Somehow, she always ended up believing the men in her life were somehow stronger, smarter, more experienced than her. In all the years as her confidant, Walter could not remember a single time in which she had chosen the man in her life. She never looked for them. They just flocked to her, and if she had nothing else to do, she would say yes, to whatever they suggested. He could remember a phone call one evening, seventeen year old Anna-Ray was sobbing. She couldn't understand how she had ended up sleeping with three different men on the same day. The married owner of the bistro she worked in, an old friend who had visited the night before and her boyfriend du jour. Her body had not enjoyed any of them. In a way she had simply felt sorry for them. She was adept at playing the benevolent whore. It seemed degrading for men to be so full of hormones, desperate for release. They became jumpy and incoherent. So in the space of twelve hours she gave one a quick blow job, bent over for the other and fell into the arms of the last, keen to make up for her slip ups, meticulously keeping score. Conversation was always better afterwards.

Walter knows Sigmund had been oblivious to all of this and he has no intention of enlightening him, this is something he means to keep for himself. An equalizer between him and the man who still has control over his sphincter muscle. They had grown up in a small town and were the same age, so it was not entirely unusual that they had shared a woman. To some extent it made it easier to bear the intimacy required to be bathed and dressed by him. He knows the male nurse to be pensive and gentle. Sigmund had taught Anna-Ray how to spin wool. The two men have become so intimate they have begun to share some of the love with each other that Anna-Ray had passed on to both of them. He had watched her love so many, as if all she needed was a target for her affection, each of them ultimately replaceable.

Session Four

Let's come away from the rainy grey of Scotland and turn towards the Netherlands. Let's go to Amsterdam. It's a brilliantly sunny autumn day. It is the 12th of September in 1936.

If you look over there, you can see the rag collector wandering the streets of Amsterdam, the wheels of his wooden cart rattle across cobblestone. From time to time he stops and calls out, his voice raw from overuse: 'Lompenjoed!' Rag Jew. Horse drawn carts overtake him leisurely, an old cat is crouched at the side of a canal, mesmerised by the glittery reflections of autumn sunlight on murky water, it smells fishy. Suddenly, the cat is startled, ducks and jumps aside. A group of boys comes running around the corner, squawking profanities as dirty as their knees – to the indignation of two elderly ladies. Two of the boys grab apples from a fruit vendor's cart and separate from the group, no good byes, no ceremony. Divide and conquer. No one is overly concerned, they know the faction.

Occasionally, even the royal children run with this horde of snot nosed urchins.

The boys sprint on, there is much to do in Amsterdam, especially if you are eight and ten years old. They are the Puschat lads, Georg and Leo. They have been told to be on time today, their mum has promised them a surprise.

The front door, never locked, flies open. There is no one in the reception room, no one in the kitchen. On the large wooden table there is a jug of cinnamon drink and some ginger bread, the boys are ravenous but they know better than to help themselves without their mother's permission. Where is she?

They creep up the stairs, to the parents' bedroom. Georg carefully opens the door. It smells funny. Their mother lies in bed, sleeping. There is a cot beside her, in itself nothing special, since it has been standing here for a while now. But this time something is moving inside; suddenly shy, he walks closer and takes a peek. A wrinkly little something looks back at him, he lets out an astonished whistle. Abruptly, the corners of its mouth are drawn down, the little chin is dimpled, it begins to whimper. Georg, now joined by his brother Leo, is stunned. That little dwarf's hair is red as fire, the colour screams louder than the bundle itself.

The brothers take a step back. 'It's a troll' whispers Leo. Their mother does not stir and after a short while the screaming changes into a muffled sob, then calm and soft breathing. The boys slowly back out of the room.

In the corridor they are met by Mevrouw Teden, the midwife. 'What are you lads doing back so early? Have you said hello to your new sister yet?' 'New sister? You mean that's a girl?' 'Well, of course, it is. And she has a name already. It is Saskia. Now boys, let's go into the kitchen, your mum has made me some snacks but I need to watch my waist.' She pats her rounded stomach. 'I don't want to offend her by leaving any, care to help?' She does not have to ask twice.

Later that afternoon, the urchin horde storms the bedroom, led by Leo, who wants to show off his weird new sister. His mum manages a smile and it is only when he starts to squeeze the little head, declaring it to be just like a coconut that her dark eyes change from gentle glow to furious glower. The crowd is swiftly bellowed out. Frouwkje Puschat, née Walda, is a born Friesian. With her small beady eyes, thin lips and black hair she does not live up to the stereotype of a Dutch woman. She is forever surrounded by a hint of Eau de Cologne and even now she is wearing a hair piece and lip stick. Her shortness emphasises a magnificent bosom, which shelters a chafed heart that, despite its soft insulation, has lost its warmth.

Her husband Heinrich Puschat, however, has the looks of a movie star. This unfortunate circumstance leads to frequent domestic disputes, not helped by the fact that he works for a chain of grocery stores and has to travel the entirety of the Netherlands. He decorates store windows, makes them look attractive. He knows how to advertise and sell. A true gentleman from head to the silver tip of his cigarette holder. Is it his fault that women's knees fall open at the sesame mellow of his voice?

Apart from these tiny interruptions the family is not badly off. They live on the ground floor of a spacious rental apartment in the heart of Amsterdam, with plenty to eat and everyone in good health. There is even a small terrier, which, equipped with basket and note, can fetch the paper from the corner shop or the odd nutmeg from the grocer's. Who, in such Waltonian bliss, would worry about vicious rumours of political unrest that seem to pollute the atmosphere like a persistent bad smell? Baby Saskia is not paying attention to politics. She is far too busy growing, counting and re-counting her toes, filling endless amounts of nappies and screaming the house down. As a result of her efforts she sleeps right through her father's brilliant idea.

Neither Saskia nor her curly red hair can be tamed. Her mother Frouwkje is busy with the new baby sister Annegret, all blond and sweetness. Her dad remains a distant and shapeless figure, whose arms scoop her up and drop her all at once, his hurried kisses smell of tobacco and oil paints. At four years old she runs out of the house, jumps onto the tram in Amsterdam, lurks in front of the school house, learning as she listens to the teacher's voice while crouching under the windowsill. Education is hard to come by at her age and there is much she can't understand.

On her way home there is excitement everywhere. Men are marching. They are dressed wonderfully, and their singing is from another world. Saskia is spellbound. A spectator lifts her onto his shoulders so she can see the show. He explains to her these are *moffen*, Germans, and there is a tone in his voice that you find hard to interpret. He doesn't sound angry, there is a sadness. It sounds a bit like her mum when she tells them their father will once again not be home. So those are Germans. They look nice. There are flags, there are crowds, there is music, shiny boots and sweets.

When she comes home her father is using language she has never heard before, wonderful words that roll off her tongue although they result in clips around her ears.

After this day the children are frequently left at home. Even Saskia is shaken when she cowers in her bedroom, clutching the screaming bundle Annegret, thunderous bombs falling in the distance. Bombs thrown by the English, who have come to save Saskia and her family, but, according to her father, their so-called allies couldn't fucking aim their own piss into a bucket. It is soon decided that Frouwkje needs a rest and the children a firmer hand. Along with her brothers and baby sister, Saskia is sent to stay with her grandmother, who runs a tight farm on a West Friesian island. No tractors in those days, no fancy kitchen machines, no cuddles for the little ones. The horses are for work only, they are giant Friesian heifers. The boys are recruited to help in the fields. Saskia, too small to help, is mainly in the way, eyes wide open, watching as her grandmother swiftly decapitates chickens, marvels as they flutter on, headless.

In the evenings the girls are locked up in their beds, small alcoves in the wall, sealed with heavy oak doors. Children should be neither seen nor heard, but most of all they need to be kept out of earshot of the farmhands' less than clean language.

Saskia kicks against the thick wooden doors, she shouts, she wails, she revolts against darkness and injustice; proves that she knows plenty of foul language already, but sparks outrage only in her brother Leo. One evening he exchanges the grainy yellow substance from the mustard pots against the grainy yellow substance from his baby sister's nappy. He can't sit for a week but his act of civil disobedience will give him the backbone he needs to withstand what's coming.

Session Six

Deep breath, make sure you are warm enough, you are once again off to Scotland, up to that hill in Langholm NOW, where nine men and a solicitor are gathering, remember?

A car slowly crawls up the narrow path, too small to carry the coffin but safe enough to bring Gerald, a man whose stony face is betrayed by the redness around his eyes. Yes, he is late, let them think what they want. If he has to attend this farce he is going to do it in his own time, on his terms.

Had he locked the front door? Protection, this was what she had never understood. He had been protecting her. The danger always came from the outside, she could not see that, for her it was within. Anna-Ray was gone and he has been deprived of a chance to say I told you so.

Along with her his right arm has gone missing, or rather the need for it. His armpit had served as a hiding place for her face when they cuddled up in front of television, his muscles stopped her from falling. She had claimed her synaesthesia had made it hard for her to watch horror films, she could taste the victim's blood and smell the fear. It never occurred to him that she stayed with him on that sofa not because she wanted to watch the film, but because the demons that slithered inside her head when she was lying in bed alone, realising he wasn't coming up to be with her, were so much more unnerving.

He parks the car carefully, at sufficient distance from the fence to ensure no animal would come close to scratching the veneer. He locks the doors, then pulls the handle of the driver's door, once, twice, three times. Walks around to the back, checks the boot, walks around to the front, checks the lock on the passenger door, once, twice, three times. He then has to look inside making sure the little LED of the car alarm is blinking his way into freedom. One more time, driver's door, boot, passenger door, once, twice, three times. And one more time, yes, the light is blinking. He feels the sudden urge to jump back inside his shell, airbag, impact protection, safety glass. But instead he turns around and faces the extraordinary gathering of men, watching him, curious, bemused with his rituals. Why is he not leaving? Why does he feel he has no choice in the matter? Has he checked the locks? He can feel his heart jump into his constricted throat, struggling for breath. How dare she tar him with the same brush?

They had met on the internet, on a dating site. Tentative email exchanges at first; she had liked that he had responded although she had not sent a photo. Texting followed, then phone calls. She did not particularly like his voice, she sensed he spoke in a higher pitch than natural, as if he had run out of conversation and had to squeeze the leftovers past his throat like toothpaste. "You can meet me now or you can wait" she had emailed him. "But if you don't want to wait you will have to meet me in Venice." His spontaneous response had revealed the details for his flight, including price of booking. They had met on the Rialto Bridge and by the time they spotted each other in the crowd her need for romance had drowned out her sense of calamity and they crossed over into a new beginning, she did not know that most of their time together would be a dance on eggshells. After all, he had come all this way. Her hair was as short as her skirt. That first warm summer night the moonlight surfed on the Canale Grande underneath. She leaned over the edge, he stood behind her, his arms already wrapping her to go. She turned her head and leaned back, attempting to get a better view of his face, and he kissed her, surprised by his own pluckiness. Musicians had placed candles along the side of the bridge, a lonely tramp played the violin beautifully. How many lovers had joined the tableau on this stage over time? "For fuck's sake" she said, "all that's missing is a bloody dove and I swear I will throw up." Both laughed when a scabby pigeon landed in front of them on one malformed leg and inspected the couple, head tilted.

But let's come back to our funeral scene. Finally, a hearse. It struggles up the path, at every bump they can see the coffin jump up a little, as if even now, she is trying to run. She had bruised so easily. Oh well, not that it mattered now. Gerald felt his heart muscle thumping harder. His palms turn sweaty and he consciously has to remind himself to push his shoulders down. Fight or flight response, a sabre tooth tiger jumping out at a cave man, in terms of evolution our bodies have not changed much since then. He knew the theory. Breathe in two three hold, out two three four hold, in two three hold, out two three four hold. Shoulders down. Thick veins on his forehead guide little beads of sweat onto his brows. His stomach churns.

Halfway up the final stretch, the hearse slows down, engine revving. Would they have to carry her up? No, the final hurdle is overcome, the black vehicle crawls on towards them. It is driven by her solicitor.

Session Seven

It is time to check on the progress of little Grant, the miner's son. So we jump back to Durham in 1930. I get a sense you are not yet fully immersed in the atmosphere of this place, so let's really push the cliché this time. Let's white wash time and call it laundry day.

It is Monday and that makes it the most exhausting day of the week. A Geordie wife takes pride in the cleanliness of her house. Mary has been commandeered to polish all brass parts in the kitchen, using ash from the stove, mixed with water. Her older sister Tiny is dragging a bucket with brushes and cloths. It will take hours to scrub the cast iron oven and blacken it up again, rubbing oil into all nooks and crannies.

Jack, the oldest, is nineteen and helps with the men down the Dolly pit. Little Grant helps his mother to press pieces of laundry through the wooden mangle, squeezing every drop of water from the fabric after she has beaten and twisted it with the Poss stick in a tub full of soapy water and scrubbed it on the washboard. Can you smell the soap, made of crushed bone? The wet linen?

> *'You could tell a Monday morning*
> *By the rhyme of the beat.*
> *You could hear a thousand poss-tubs,*
> *Echo down the street,*
>
> *You could tell a Monday morning,*
> *By the drumming of the stick.*
> *Thrashing out the washing,*
> *Muckied through the week.*
>
> *You could tell a Monday morning,*
> *Such a day of toil.*
> *Stoken up the set-pot,*
> *Te-get the water on the boil.*
>
> *You could tell a Monday morning,*
> *By a call across the wall.*
> *"Come an-twine-me mangle Meg,*

So the Blankets dinnet fall. "

You could tell a Monday morning,
They hoped it wouldn't rain.
Sooty smoke whirled in the air,
Soapy bubbles down the drain.

You could tell a Monday morning,
Getting close to noon,
When the tyhump of all those poss-tubs,
Began to settle down.
You could tell a Monday morning,
With the lines across the street
All the washing hanging there, Spotless, clean and
neat. '

The five year old has to hurry to keep up, his mum tends to stomp and beat laundry in the rhythm of the old Geordie chant, loud rather than beautiful. The little hands push inch after inch of cloth between the heavy wooden rolls of the mangle. While the right hand turns the wheel, the left hand pushes. The squeezed liquid is caught in a small drain, runs back into the trough.

Grant loves the kitchen. During the day this is where life takes place. At night it becomes his parents' bedroom, so the children can share the chamber upstairs. During supper the children are expected to stay silent, so his father can discuss the events of the day with his wife. And sometimes, but only when he is in this very special mood, John lights a pipe, makes himself comfortable in the big chair and is quickly surrounded by his three younger ones, while his oldest pretends to read the paper. In those moments the children's mouths fall open as he conjures up blood dripping from battle axes, courageous heroes and peel towers with walls as thick as their garden long. He speaks of the good old days of the Armstrongs, when they were a respected riding clan, unruly and notorious Border reivers. Sometimes he speaks of their friends, the Elliotts, and their enemies, the sheriffs of Carlisle, he whispers of treachery and deceit.

He speaks of Archibald Armstrong, who was sentenced to death and who requested his hanging to be postponed until after he had read in the bible. When this was granted he confessed he could not read and had no intention of learning to. The King was so amused he made Archibald court jester.

He speaks of Kinmont Willie Armstrong, who promised not to run away when captured by the Sheriff of Carlisle, so his men broke into the castle grounds and carried him away.

He speaks of baptising a baby with its right hand sticking out of the water, so, once grown up, it could wield a sword with clear conscience. Of the way in which a reiver's wife would leave a pair of spurs on her husband's plate instead of cooking tea – a gentle hint it was time to reive some shopping. He explains how the word bereaved came from the reivers, as well as blackmail, and how thoroughly the Armstrongs had been cursed by the archbishop of Glasgow.

"I curse their head and all the hairs of their head; I curse their face, their brain, their mouth, their nose, their tongue, their teeth, their forehead, their shoulders, their breast, their heart, their stomach, their back, their womb, their arms, their legs, their hands, their feet, and every part of their body, from the top of their head to the soles of their feet, before and behind, within and without.

May all the plagues that fell upon Pharaoh and his people of Egypt, their lands, crops and cattle, fall upon them, their equipment, their places, their lands, their crops and livestock.

And may all the vengeance that ever was taken since the world began, for open sins, and all the plagues and pestilence that ever fell on man or beast, fall on them for their openly evil ways, senseless slaughter and shedding of innocent blood."

Grant's father is a great storyteller. When he speaks, he acts the voices and can rapidly change from booming baritone to falsetto if needed.

'Now, Alexander, Laird of Mangerton, we have a special surprise for you. You have enjoyed the main, may you revel in the dessert! Laughter, loud laughter roars. An arm wipes bowls and plates aside – and before the eyes of the Laird the freshly severed head of a black bull is **slammed** (he slams his hand on the table, the children jump) on the stone table. Flies circle the bloody cut. Alexander has been warned. But, before his hand can reach his weapon, the ice cold steel of the Soulis family enters his neck. Since then, children, the Soulis have been the arch enemies of the Armstrongs. Remember that!' 'What happened to Soulis, Dad?' 'Well, lad, he was stuck in a barrel of boiling lead until his flesh fell from his bones.'

Sadly, his father is not often in the mood for the old stories and he will not allow the children to ask for them. Grant is lost in the stories in his head and turns the wheels of the mangle until his small arms become heavy as lead.

Back at laundry day he is about to ask his mother how many more sheets they need to squeeze and flatten when a bottle of half fermented raspberry wine explodes on the shelf. Juice splashes over the stone tiled floor and Grant instinctively ducks to avoid the glass shards. Before he realises, one of his fingers is trapped between the rollers, and with a terrible scrunching noise the tip is crushed, blood is soaked up by the freshly scrubbed linen underneath. Mother and sisters scream louder than the victim himself. Instead of helping him they embrace him and kiss him hysterically, while the little one attempts desperately to free his finger. When he finally comes loose, they are all covered in blood and ashes, mixed with raspberry wine and soapy suds.

'What's the do?' A roaring voice disrupts the chaos. Father has returned. Grant points at the mangle; his fingernail is still stuck to the linen. Then he notices his father's look. All Armstrong, Grant takes the nail and squeezes it back onto the wound. 'Nout, Sir.'

His mother loses her taste for Raspberry wine on this day. The nail grows back.

Session Eight

We are losing track of Saskia, so let's return to Amsterdam in 1941. Saskia and her siblings have escaped the clutches of their grandmother and have been sent back to Amsterdam. But these are troubled times. No one in the Netherlands has much of anything, food is rationed. Shops are finding it hard enough to supply the essentials; they cannot afford to display perishables in their windows. Heinrich finds himself faced with the difficult task of making hundreds of grocery stores look attractive without showing anything. The Netherlands robbed of their proud wheels of cheese – unthinkable! In patriotic spirit and with the help of an affluent partner, Heinrich finally realises the great idea that he has carried with him for years now. He establishes a small company named SchilKa and starts to produce fake cheeses.

Right in the heart of Amsterdam they turn small prefabricated metal shapes into wedges of delicious dairy products, Edam, Nagel Kaas, Gouda, Leidse Kaas, smoked cheese, cream cheese, mature and extra mature, using nothing but spit, polish and yellow varnish. In order to power the engine of the polishing machine, the men take turns struggling along on an old bicycle. Their efforts are successful: soon not only Amsterdam's citizens drool over the tasty displays, which are cunningly decorated with dots of mould and little labels mocking growling stomachs with promises of 28% fat content. But the fumes of the high-pressure paint nozzles stain their neighbours' curtains yellow, People begin to complain. The factory, with family in tow, is moved to a small town called Leeuwarden. Here, they find a small flat above a garage – the ideal location for a small workshop. To begin with, the factory flourishes but soon shop owners run out of budgets for luxuries, so SchilKa begin to take on bodywork for cars as well. In the end they even paint vases. The men begin to make a profit and things are looking up. But of course you know this cannot last, and you are right. I would advise you now to take cover! When the nozzle of the spray gun clogs up, it causes an immense pressure build up in one of the gas tanks. The resulting explosion has such impact, that the roof of the building is torn away. Saskia is later told by her brother that she was found unharmed in the rubble, several rooms away from her own. While this may be a lose interpretation of the truth, one fact is irrefutable, the company is ruined. The family salvage what has not burned. They need money for a new start.

German occupying forces have built a small airport near their house. The troops behave well, they don't plunder, nor do they molest the Dutch women, the locals get used to having them around. Following the Queen's escape with her cabinet to Great Britain no one knows what to expect anymore. Heinrich uses his German skills and helps out at the airport canteen. Frouwkje helps him, but gets a little too friendly with the troops. Back at home Georg tries out how long he can hang his little sister upside down outside the attic window before she turns blue. Leo snaps little gold fish in two, one by one. Baby Annegret screams. Somewhere in Amsterdam, Anne Frank is preparing to go into hiding.

One evening the boys 'shoot' at Germans with broomstick rifles from of their bedroom window. Not a severe crime, but the soldiers have no sense of humour, they shoot back with live ammunition. Miraculously, no one is hurt.

When she is not working, Frouwkje entertains her newfound friends. Saskia watches her from the top of the stairs, flirting, drinking wine, only when daddy isn't home. One day he returns early. They fight, she tells the men that he of all people should not mind. He has German blood after all. The matter is investigated. She is right, his father came from Prussia, Puschat is a German name. He is encouraged to demonstrate his sense of patriotism and work for the German military. Many Dutch have crossed over, some even joined the Waffen SS, others simply remain silent in the light of facts they have known about all along. Neighbours have begun to disappear. Heinrich refuses, he is Dutch. For a little while he hides at his mother's house, until a Dutch village policeman feels obliged to inform the 'moffen'. Heinrich works as a human air raid detector for the Germans, then he is sent to France. As a courier in the Normandy he manages to smuggle himself away from battlefields. Instead of weapons he carries repair kits, fixes watches and investigates old castles, barters, exchanges, trades.

In the meantime his wife maintains good relations with the Germans.

After Annegret's birth her sense of maternal duty is exhausted. After all, she has had to look after her eight siblings when she was young. Her sons are not easy to handle.

One winter's night there is a knock on the door. 'Who is it?' Saskia hears her father's beloved voice answer 'Sinterklaas', father Christmas. The little girl races to the door, screaming 'Dad is home, Dad is home.' And there he is, a large bag flung over his shoulder, full of gifts. Among other luxuries he has brought Saskia a white fur coat and white satin gloves, items that will be exchanged for food before she gets a chance to wear them. Heinrich is not amused by his wife's close contact with the enemy. She laughs, after all he is the one in the German uniform. They fight, he turns around on the spot and disappears into the night.

Unsupervised, Saskia spends her days roaming the streets of Leeuwarden. One day she hears music. It seems to come from a small building. It is piano music. The little meisje has never heard such a thing. From now on she skulks around the house more and more, until someone notices her. The little house is in fact a primary school, and the man talking to her is its only teacher. He attempts to send her home, but she insists on coming back day after day. In the end Saskia, much too young, is allowed to take part in lessons. Soon she can read and write, but most of all she loves hammering the keys of the big brown piano.

Conditions worsen. Annegret screams non-stop, the airport is bombarded, the brothers are nowhere to be found. At nights sirens howl. People run to shelters, buildings collapse. Saskia watches from her bedroom window. Her mother left her alone, she is trying to watch over her baby sister. Do me a favour and go over to her. Wrap her up in your arms, shelter the two from harm. I really need you to do this now, I depend on you. When neighbours have to climb in with ladders to rescue the girls, they inform the German police. Frouwkje is volunteered to help the German war machine in the Buxtehude ammunition factory.

Leo is seventeen, he is sent to help out on the Russian front. Georg is fifteen, not old enough to serve, he disappears. Not long after, Annegret is placed with an infant's home in Zeedijk, Saskia is taken to a camp in Zijst.

Session Nine

Are you sick of war yet? I agree, you need a break. You decide to float back into the here and NOW, up in the Scottish Borders.

You will remember the solicitor had just turned up, bringing with him the coffin? After switching off the engine the man takes a moment for himself, to gather his thoughts and prepare his speech as much as to create a dramatic effect.

The men have gathered, he counts all nine. He is not sure about this, it seems in bad taste. Thankfully no one seems to have started a fight. They just stand there, silent as ghosts. The weather has softened the ground further, good, this should make their task easier, although, if memory serves him correctly, the ground in these hills is stony. Memory, nothing but an unknown quantity of synapses, executing his free will in firing randomly. Arbitrary thoughts, intrusions of his privacy, have plagued him for a while now. How, for example does he know about the synaptic connections? Where had he even learned the expression? And this job – has he checked the legality? He cannot remember. He knows he has been able to find them all, contact them, get them to come here, an unlikely success. Now it is time to get the show on the road. He steps out of the hearse.

They are not impressed with him. His witty little pun about the weather putting them under pressure was lost on them. A tough audience. But before they know what hit them he has declared her final request: she wants them to dig the grave. Maybe there is some kind of symbolism to this that escapes them. The solicitor provides all necessary equipment, pick axes, shovels, tent pegs and ropes to mark out the shape and location. The grave is to be right here, centred on the top of the hill, so the men start digging, surrounded by the parked cars, no questions asked. They are glad for the task, it takes away the obligation to exchange conversation, allowing them to communicate much more effectively in silence.

The teamwork pays off. Here they stand, lining the rectangular hole, deep enough to bury two coffins, quality work. When had they finished it? How had it turned out this neat? Had anyone been in charge? They cannot remember digging.

Ansgar is the man most stared at. Some of the mourners have already met him, some are still hoping that he is not one of them. Surely she hadn't? He did, in fact, look much older than he was. Years of mountaineering, climbing in the heat of Africa, the ice of the Himalayas and a hip replacement have turned him into a slightly bent version of a grandfather Christmas, carrying an invisible weighty sack. Flowing silver grey hair, his beard long but trimmed, she had sometimes complained that he wasn't looking after himself. I know what you are going for, she used to say, you are still trying to look like a rebellious hippie. Unfortunately, at your age, it comes across more like a wino. Wino! He had loved it when she had come up with these cute neologisms. Homeless bum then, she had explained crossly. So adorable when she was angry. Her

German accent became just a little more noticeable then. And how prophetic a profanity. With no one to snuggle up to, his bum was indeed homeless now. And a little cold in the breeze, he noticed with a shiver.

Ansgar was wearing his kilt to the funeral. Another one of those little threads designed to add to the dream coat of the man whose reflection he wanted to see in the eyes of others. Shiny reflections, like the one from the silver framed picture of a younger him, receiving a Churchill medal from Queen Mum herself, strategically placed right next to the entrance of his eternally under heated house. A slight whiff of fungus from corners behind the piano. There is damp, she had told him as soon as she had entered his house for the first time. She could smell the damage years before he could.

Not long before she met him he had given up on life. He told her how he had peaked, had mounted too many summits and women. There had been plenty regrets, not enough recognition for his efforts. He had sat there at his kitchen table, the content of four boxes of pills neatly lined up in front of him. Citalopram, Nembutal, Diazepam, Vicodin, a mug of hot tea with milk, no sugar. After he had spent an eternity popping each pill out of the silver dispenser packaging he had created little patterns on the shiny table surface, a boy with smarties. Down here at the bottom of his well he could see no light, he hummed and could hear the echo in the hollow of his chest. Blow the hot tea, sip, pick a pill, swallow. Blow, sip, pick, swallow. As a mountaineer, he had a habit of pacing himself, placing one foot in front of the other in slow determination. He was often passed by other climbers to begin with, the same guys he would greet when passing them hours later. His eyes firmly on the ground he never failed to reach the top, missing the view on his way up. The tea ran out before the pills, he had to get up and make another cup. There was no desperation in him, no sense of urgency. The kitchen tiles were greasy, he noticed on his way to the floor, and before he passed out he recognised a glimmer of embarrassment about this detail. He should have cleaned the place first. What else would they find when they rummaged through his things? When he came round he was surprised to feel a sense of relief.

He had always felt eighteen and still had to brace himself before looking into a mirror. Who was that old man staring back? Bags under his eyes, turkey neck, even his big ears – a sign of intelligence – were now separated from his face by severe vertical lines.

Countless women in countless countries had fallen for his persistence before his charms. But he had been handsome then. Lean, the beard still red, a spark in the eye, always hungry for skin. She had fallen for him as he was now.

She could love what he could not accept. Nothing he had found repulsive about himself had deterred her. They had shared intimacies, he hadn't even bothered hiding his false teeth after a while. She had never understood that this had been her gift to him. She had always claimed to be his trophy girlfriend. 'Cut off my head - display it on your mantle piece' she had written in exchange of one of his love poems. In allowing him to feel her she had resuscitated the eighteen year old inside. He had come alive. She had held him when he was low, she had unbuttoned her blouse and let him drink from her breasts, which he did, greedily sucking until he felt strong and she was weak and empty. When he had sucked her hollow, he neatly folded up her empty skin and locked her inside a wooden box, but not before explaining the historical significance of the carvings.

Ansgar steps forward and assumes his place at the head of the open grave, his bent back underlining his grief over losing her again, losing all chance of reconciliation. After the separation she had told him many times that she was not, not ever, going to consider any form of contact, let alone friendship or more, another effort to transmit beyond his frequency range. He clears his throat. 'Anna means favour or grace. Ray means wise protector. This is how she came to favour me.' Scanning the crowd with that schoolboy pride he continues, an invisible headmaster's pat on the back. 'We met at a Burn's supper. It was a match made in the head of a mutual friend.' It had taken him hours to come up with that line. 'She had told me when she invited me that Anna-Ray was beautiful, but she hadn't told me how incredible she really was. She had the most amazing smile, the smoothest skin, the wickedest sense of humour. She was never cross, she was an amazing lover and she had the most brilliant mind I have ever had the pleasure to...' '..fuck.' came a voice from the mourner's crowd. The old man looks up, hurt.

Ansgar had known, of course. She had tried to tell him more or less from the start. The signs had all been there. At first she had been shy, avoiding his touch. Once, during a walk along the river he had attempted to hold her hand. He had tried to make it seem casual but she had pulled away as if he had beaten her. Hiding her hands in her pockets she had mumbled something about 'cold hands'. She had been coy, the little minx, playing hard to get. He had known she was eccentric from the start, ever since she had told him she lived on top of a hill in the borders, in a little old cottage, hidden away. Great legs under that dress. She had been too young for that kind of life, what would make a woman like that move into utter solitude with a small child? He had been intrigued. Having climbed some of the highest mountains this hill had needed to be worn away gradually. She had let him visit, always waiting with coffee, she had introduced him to frothy milk. But she had never once flirted, cleverly disguising the fact she wanted him. In the end he had been unprepared when she had finally allowed him to kiss her. It was then that she had known they had something in common, tasting another woman's cunt juice in his beard. He was a slut, as much as she was.

At what point had she told him about the fantasies? He had demanded her night after night, she had obliged him. He could tell he pleased her, he knew she wanted him. She had told him more than once she needed him. How lonely she had been on that hill. He had courted her like the man he longed to be, for nine long weeks he had written poems, cards, had told her about his far away adventures, bought flowers and cheap wine. He hadn't known she didn't drink then. When he was with her he could hardly hear the critic in his head. What have you achieved in your life? Nothing, I tell you, nothing. You are not rich, you are living on a pension, you couldn't even manage to keep your marriages together. Others have published books, they have travelled places you have never seen, they have purpose. The Royal Geographical Society send you invites but they don't know who you are. Do you think the Queen Mum remembers you? Determined to leave a mark he wanted to push her into success but she resisted. Her child then. Her son needed music lessons, needed to learn to dress properly. He knew his way round in certain circles, he had connections. If he played their cards right, he, no they, could make it after all. He just had to be tough enough. No child would learn not to make his mistakes if he wasn't stitched in time. There was real potential here. He smelled salvation.

One night, away skiing in the Alps, he had proven how much he loved her. He had missed her so much, couldn't bear that she could not accompany him on his trip for something as trivial as financial reasons. He would have loved to pay for her stay, too, but, knowing of her pride, had decided against it. He had been on the phone to her the sixth time that night when the connection ended abruptly.

Knowing she would never hang up on him he had become instantly and demonstrably terrified. There must have been a sinister reason, maybe she was in danger. He had dialled the number again, no reply. He had tried again, then another time, no reply still. What if someone had broken into the cottage, she was alone up there. What if she was in danger, with him so far away? It had taken him a while to find out the number of a police station near her.

It was dark when she woke. She froze instantly. A car was driving up her hill, slowly but at constant speed, as if to avoid the noise of a revving engine. No one ever came up here at night. Hers was the only house this far up and she was not in the habit of receiving visitors after midnight. Hiding in the dark, she peaked out of her bedroom window. She could see the car now. No headlights. This was bad. Who would drive up a hill in the middle of the night, silently, no lights? Oh please, she thought, not again. She knew there was nowhere to hide. The house was old, the windows so frail they could be opened with no more than a violent tug. The front door was locked but made of old wood, decorated with a glass pane that made the heavy bolt a mockery. Had she even bothered closing it before she went to bed? She could hear the car doors slam, footsteps, more than one person, around the house. Torch lights shining into the windows. Just burglars? Or worse? Local lads who found out the young German woman was living all on her own up there? If it was her they were after she should go outside now, get it over with. No need to endanger the child. She could feel her heart beat in the tip of her tongue. Missing a beat. And a thump in her chest. Missing a beat. Another thump. Thump thump thump, this time on the front door. 'Police, open up please.'

What the...? She sneaked towards the side of the front door. What did people say in American films when this happened? 'Show me some ID.' And there it was, pressed against the glass pane. As if she could tell the difference. By the time she decided to open the door she knew what this was about. While she was showing the officers around her house, checking behind doors for hidden intruders that may have severed her phone cord, it dawned on her that the old man really did love her. Loved her in a way she had never been loved before. This one would protect her, would never leave her, was incapable of harming her. And while she was trying to calm her startled son, who was still shaken by the unexpected sight of two policemen entering his bedroom in the middle of the night it occurred to her that the old man was exactly what she needed. She couldn't love, but she could be loved.

Her gift in return had come cheap. It was only her body, a useless lump of meat, an accumulation of bones, skin, blood and an increasing quantity of body fat. A mass that could be moved in skilled ways, robbing thankfulness from his lips, thieving warmth from his embrace. When she had finally told him about her secret, she had been devastated, crying for his forgiveness. Maybe she ought not to have told him, she had sobbed. Maybe she could take it back. Take it back? How? How could one undo thoughts? Her thoughts when she had been with him, his memory of her confession. Whenever he had touched her after that he had done it knowingly, no longer ignorant of the images in her head. He had become an accomplice. She had left him, had gone away to Venice, where she met someone else and he had fallen back into his black hole.

She had gone back on her promise to stay with him, to look after him, to hold him when he died. He was so much older than her, it had always been clear to him that he was going to go before her. But here he was, at Anna-Ray's funeral, having to face these men, these lovers.

Silence, a few suppressed coughs. 'My friend and I sang at that supper, a little something written by Robert Burns, a song, which, I feel, is most befitting for this sad moment.' Ignoring the look of panic on the faces of his fellow mourners, Ansgar clears his throat and begins, with the skilled falsetto of a former choir boy.

> Ae fond kiss – and then we sever.
> Ae farewell, alas, forever.
> With heartwrung tears I pledge thee
> Weary sighs and groans I wage thee...
> Had we never kissed sae kindly

Had we never loved sae blindly

Never kissed and never parted

We would ne'er been broken hearted.

He lingers on that last note, at the final tremolo his voice broke and he starts sobbing inconsolably, with real snot running from his nostrils into his white moustache.

'Now that was a fucking load of wank.' That voice again. Ansgar freezes. He abhors profanities. Whenever he had argued with Anna-Ray he had told her he wasn't going to listen to her unless she used proper language.

Session Ten

And back in time you go, back to Durham, in 1935, checking on little Grant's progress. We are behind the school house of Dipton.

'To seik het water beneath cauld ice – surely it was a great follie. I hae asked grace at a graceless face.' 'Pah, Johnnie Armstrong, these were your last words. How dare you mock death itself? See now how we punish your audashyness. You will be hanged with all your men!' Thomas, son of the butcher, looks truly spine chilling in the role of cruel James IV. Grant stands on top of a heap of earth. He loves reciting the laird of Mangerton's famous last words. His Scottish dialect is a little tainted by his Geordie upbringing, but girls in the area love that mix. It's exotic. 'Hang him, men!' Thomas throws himself against the much younger boy. Instead of dying slowly yet dramatically, Grant hits back. He pummels Thomas with well aimed hits.

'Grant, stop, it's only a game!' Shocked by this interference the small hero looks up: 'Mary, stop meddling. These are the affairs of men.' His sister snubs this meek attempt at being dominant and points at his school books, carelessly tossed aside. 'Well, you will need your courage to face the teacher at school tomorrow when you show him this. I am not covering for you anymore.' She collects the books. 'Come now, Jack is home already.' Grant nods, gives Thomas a quick push, then he trots after his sister.

For a while now the family has lived in the valley. Far away from the terraced cottages of the mining families. A shape appears in the distance, leaning on a walking stick. Mary blushes. 'Oh my god, I forgot about granddad.' Old Joseph Armstrong has turned completely blind. Sometimes Mary takes him out onto the green, but it is not the first time she has forgotten about him over a game with neighbour's kids, or chasing after her brother. The old man may be blind, but he remains the highest authority in the family. It is he who insists that the children are to wear only proper clothing. Despite the meagre income from the pits, the children in this family never wear hand me downs. Thomasina has to mend clothes in secret. She may not have that Armstrong pride but she certainly is practical.

In the evenings Jack has made it a habit to take his younger brother out for a stroll in the forest. With the use of a provisional ring made from sticks and washing line, he teaches him everything he knows about boxing. Grant is already slightly taller than Jack, a fact that causes concern.

If he continues to grow at this rate he will not fit into the pit shafts.

Grant does not mind. His ambitions are taking a different turn. He wants to be a warrior. When his sister Tiny is engaged to a soldier of the Durham Light Infantry, Grant secretly tries on his uniform and takes a long hard look in the mirror. Tiny, who surprises the little plumped up cockerel, bursts out laughing. She causes a wound that will smart for over thirty years, when he burns his regimental kilt, after his wife, who has never seen a man in a skirt, laughs in exactly the same way.

Session Eleven

Yes, that's right, you are back in the moment, back to NOW, at the gathering at Upper Caulfield. You may remember the rude interruption of Ansgar's speech? It turns out the voice of the heckler belongs to Gunther, another old man. Oh my god, had she really been such a coffin snatcher? This guy is not too handsome either, bald, slightly plump, lips cut into his face. In fact, he looks an awful lot like the medical hologram on the spaceship Voyager, that dreadful American filth Anna-Ray used to watch. Please state the nature of the medical emergency.

Another educated man, a professor of philosophy. He has written several very long books of the deeply intellectual and politically influential kind, the kind that passes any critique because no one, not even the author, wants to admit to not actually having read it.

With a surprising amount of passion he spits his words into the old man's face. 'I don't know who you were talking about, but it wasn't Anna-Ray.' 'Oh, and I suppose you could do better, could you?' The old man's cheeks have turned dark red. Unfortunately this makes him look even more like Santa Claus. 'I think I bloody well can', snaps the professor, pushing the surprised speaker out of the way. 'I knew her before she came to this country.'

This man is used to being centre of attention. Acting has always been his secret passion; instead, he has chosen the political stage of education. He is an influential man, with an air of authority. After countless interviews he is used to filling lecture halls to the brim with students hanging on his thin lips. 'She was never a goddess. She was an insecure young woman who did everything she was told. She was servile and very feminine but also incredibly immature. She was the kind of woman who would get abused and raped. She was a health hazard to me – to us. But I don't need to tell you that. We all know what she died of, don't we?' 'I know who you are now', Ansgar interrupts him. 'You are the pervert.' 'Excuse me?' 'You are the guy who was into S&M, aren't you? The guy who used her as a slave?'

They had met in Hamburg, on a hot sunny day. With a breeze, one should add. This is an important detail, considering that, without the breeze, the professor would not have prepared his sailing boat for launch. She wouldn't have passed on her way home from the radio station. They would not have talked. She would not have been surprised at his interest in her, despite wearing glasses and no makeup. He would never have invited her onto his boat for a quick spin across the Alster, the lake that stretches right across Hamburg's town centre. He would never have walked her through Jena park, her feet naked. She had been so spontaneous, had thrown away her shoes, allowing his arms around her right away. She had ended up jumping into a pond that afternoon, splashing, laughing.

There is a photograph to bear evidence of that day, they sit on a bench, her hair is short, just recovering from being shaven bald a few weeks earlier. Gunther has one arm around her and she is smiling. His other arm stretched forward to hold the camera, his smile is triumphant, never noticing that at that very second her left foot, blistered from the walk and naked under the bench, is sinking into a warm soft pile of canine excrement. He doesn't know that she is thinking it must have been a small dog to manage this under the bench. An efficient little German dog. Vorsprung durch Technik. Hoping he wouldn't notice the smell she had jumped straight into the nearest shallow pond, laughing with embarrassment.

Making love had been out of the question from the start. One can sense love, smell it, taste it, detest it and lose it, but one cannot make love without the basic ingredients. She had, at this point, given up on love. Intercourse, however, merely required being a mammal. And she remembered Neruda: No quiero que te vayas, dolor, ultima forma de amar. Don't leave me, pain, only form of loving. Plus, she had preserved an extraordinary curiosity about how far her quest would push her. Did she really have no boundaries at all? Was she that fucked up? Was pain the way to wake up this dead body?

The professor, himself an accomplished heckler, does not take kindly to being interrupted. 'Pervert? I don't see how this has anything to do with you. It's private. But since we are on the subject, you did the same, didn't you? You knew that she was looking for a father, she didn't come close enough with me, he had to be British, didn't he?'

Ansgar is startled. How can this man know about that? She had been with the professor before him. How dare he take the part of persecutor?

The other men around the grave are not as respectful an audience as the professor's students. Two menacing looking young men make their way towards him. One of them a young body builder type who might as well have stepped out of a Davidoff ad, the other a George Clooney twin. 'She was not a health hazard, you arsehole, and no, I don't know what she died of', said the Davidoff ad, whose actual name was Lothar. 'We haven't been told yet.' 'Who the fuck are you?' snaps the professor. 'Oh, don't tell me.

You are that young colleague of hers, aren't you? The one she was screwing while she saw me?' 'That's where you're wrong', replied Lothar. 'I was not the one. She screwed both of us, Erwin, me and you.' 'Q.E.D.', smirks the professor, wisely omitting the fact that it was he who had suggested keeping the relationship 'open'. 'You know as well as we do what happened', interjects Clooney's twin Erwin. 'She always kept us in the loop.'

Lothar had been her colleague when she was pregnant. With Ferdinand as her husband she had felt rejected, bloated, ugly. Lothar had eyed her up from day one. He had not ignored her belly, he had observed and commented on the growth of her now enormous breasts, how her legs were still shapely, her lips still full. In front of anyone who would listen he had elaborated on how it would feel to kiss her. After her child was born, her husband had not changed. He had now moved into a separate bedroom, making his decision to remain celibate final. When Anna-Ray took her mother out for coffee she confessed her dejection. It was a small café in the centre of a major book store. As usual they had chosen hot chocolate and blueberry muffins. 'He doesn't touch you at all?' her mother had exclaimed. 'He is not gay? You mean he doesn't want to go to counselling, doesn't want to change this? How does he suggest you solve this one? You are twenty-eight, for crying out loud. This is a crime, a crime, that's what it is. I tell you something', she was shouting louder now and heads were turning. 'You go out there and you get yourself a lover and pronto!' Anna-Ray had to laugh, she knew exactly who to chose, and he was not among the now alert looking men at the neighbouring table.

When she planned the rendezvous with her colleague, she had spun her husband a tall tale of wanting to see Mozart's requiem at the Hamburg Michel, a large cathedral in the city centre. Instead she met Lothar at his apartment, there was no pretence. He had a water bed, this amused her. She hesitated to take off her clothes, what if her husband was right? She had lost the weight again, but what about the crescent shaped stretch marks? Her breasts were still full of milk, would he be able to handle that? He assisted her, and in returning the favour she soon had hard evidence that her husband had been mistaken. Afterwards, she could not untie the knot from one of her stockings. They were lying on his water bed together, when he suddenly jumped up and ran into the bathroom. 'What's wrong?' she shouted but no answer came. Anna-Ray rolled herself off the bed rather ungracefully now she knew there was no audience, and walked towards the bathroom door. A distinct smell told her it was his bowel, not her presence, that had caused his sudden departure. Groaning noises. 'Can I get you anything?' More groaning, followed by frequent flushing. 'I am okay, just go back to bed, don't worry about me. I have IBS, this happens sometimes, I will be fine in a minute.' Not knowing what to do she returned into the bedroom, when she caught a glimpse of herself in the mirrored wardrobe door. The hair on the back of her head stood as one huge birds nest. 'Do you have a comb?' she shouted, but then she remembered his shaven head and was glad he had not heard her. Maybe a fork? The kitchen was kept less than immaculate but cutlery was easy to find, in a drawer underneath the sink. It took a long time to comb the knots out of her hair and by the time she finished she realised she had heard neither groaning nor flushing for quite some time.

'Are you okay? She shouted again. No reply. This time she opened the bathroom door and found him lying on the cold floor tiles, knees drawn up into foetal position, mouth open, eyes shut. She checked his pulse, there was a faint heart beat. He was breathing. Moving his tall muscular body into recovery was not easy in this tiny bathroom and she felt slightly worried about placing his head on faint yellow stains on the white floor tiles underneath the toilet. Just when she was about to leave him and call an ambulance he came round again. 'Oh, fuck, I passed out again, didn't I?' She nodded and for the first time noticed her pulse racing so fast, her breath could not catch up. 'It's the pain' he explained. 'I never know when this is going to happen or what triggers it. I am so sorry, this was not a great way to end the date, right?' 'I am glad you are ok', she smiled. When they stepped into the night air she noticed how much she smelled of his strong aftershave. This would not do. They spent a full hour sitting in a smoky bar to try and mask the scent. When she returned home, her husband did not notice her stocking missing, nor her peculiar hair style. Her marriage was over. Her affair with Lothar continued, despite the fact he could not take his eyes off his own perfect body. He was a good lover, considerate, passionate, it was easy to forgive his lack of vocabulary. The more they made love, they more she despised her own imperfections. He did not eat regular meals, instead he devoured a muculent grey wheat paste half an hour after every workout. She found steroid ampoules in his cupboard, he was holding them for a friend. His life revolved around sex, work and keeping weights up and his own weight down. He was determined not to be ill.

Anna-Ray had no intention of taking up more than the space allocated to her. Her own life was filled with parenting, work and her other two men. She argued that an ordinary housewife in an average marriage probably had more sex than her. On weekends when the child stayed with her ex, she arranged to see either Lothar or Gunther. When she was starved of culture, she went out with Erwin, a married friend, who, after awkward attempts to avoid this, had finally become her lover also. All three men were aware of each other, and none of them liked the arrangement. But, in light of the fact that none of them was willing to commit fully to this single mother, they grudgingly resigned to filling otherwise threadbare hours with her company.

Like a criminal returning to the scene of her crime she had rented the penthouse on the top floor of the registry office in Hamburg, the same building in which she had been married for the second time years earlier. Her wages from various sources were not bad, if somewhat unreliable. The occasional radio job paid the rent, engagements as a supporting actress covered food and electricity, voice-overs for documentaries and automated phone services took care of the rest. The centre piece of the apartment was a huge lounge, she needed wide open spaces, a typical northern German trait. Being raised in flat landscapes made a person grow accustomed to a life with a view. Whenever she came home she had to walk across petals to enter the building, some days rice, but more often just those tacky metal cut

outs of horseshoes and pink hearts – a never ending stream
of wedding leftovers, she had become Miss Havisham.

The heart of the lounge was a massive four-poster
bed, with beige canvas curtains that were always closed. Not
so much a personal habit but a necessity, as one wall of this
room was entirely made of glass, overlooking the skyline of
Hamburg. Some mornings would wake her with the noise of
heavy rain. She used to open the curtains a tiny bit then,
allowing the world a glimpse of her private life in exchange
for the soothing motion picture of heavy rain drops hitting
the rooftops beneath like miniature water bombs, exploding
their load onto the jagged edge of terracotta tiles,
transforming them into a jellied mass. She could smell the
wetness and feel the impact of the heavy water on her skin
just watching. Occasionally, she shared this bed with her
married friend Erwin, his wife believed him to be on
business trips. When he first told her that he suffered from
insomnia, she had felt enormous relief at being able to share
her waking hours. Whispered telephone conversations
turned into late night trips to jazz clubs along the

Reeperbahn. He was already lying about his whereabouts, when he showed her his office at four o'clock in the morning, she told him to sit in his desk chair, then crawled underneath it on hands and knees. When she unzipped his trousers she was met with a fishy smell, but the curtain had been raised and the act required her to bravely soldier on. After that she made it a habit to keep a bottle of malt whisky next to her bed. She would rinse her mouth, then let the liquid trickle onto his half open lips.

Professor Gunther, visited when her son stayed with his dad. He liked to follow a certain ritual. She would be prepared, dressed immaculately under her formal wear. A meal would stand on the table, waiting for him. He would take a seat and carefully place a leather whip onto the table, indicating his choice of dessert. Sometimes she would take him up on the offer, sometimes she would not, giving herself the illusion of free will. Games in leather were fashionable in Hamburg then, she was really only following the mainstream. It wasn't as if either of them needed these rituals, they could have had simple old fashioned nights, too. They were not like these perverts they met at parties, who depended on the toys to get off, or who went for the serious stuff like drinking urine or piercing their flesh.

Unlike Erwin and Lothar he didn't mind her secret, the images in her head were safe with him. So what if she saw him as a father trying to fuck her. She had made it very clear that it wasn't actually her father. She had never really known him anyway. It was the generic image of a father. He had read about that once. The Electra complex. All women fantasised about screwing their fathers. It was perfectly straightforward, nothing to worry about. What a good little girl you are. You can take in all that? Daddy is so proud of you. You make daddy so happy. I love you so much. She was very flexible, physically and morally. She had stopped eating food, replaced it with grey wheat gruel, and she worked out almost every night, so her body, apart from the semi circular stretch marks on her lower abdomen, was flawless. She could crawl on her knees like a panther and the tight leather straps of her bra and pants found no body fat to cut into. When the soft strips of the leather whip deceptively caressed, then swiftly struck her skin, she arched her back in response, begging him to stop, just as he liked it. She licked her lips and opened wide on command, her neck was slim and long, when he pulled her towards him tugging at the leash, she fought the collar just long enough to arouse his interest. Only when she told him about her brother did he begin to feel uncomfortable. What if she went psycho on him? His reputation would not be able to suffer a blow like that. Maybe it was time to move on.

Session Twelve

You are somewhere in Germany. It is 1943. At seven years old, Saskia Puschat is now one of the pack of stray dogs. That's what they call the children of German heritage, whose parents, usually enemies of the state, are absent. In the children's re-education camps it is forbidden to speak any language other than German. Little chatterbox Saskia becomes Sissy, the sullen quiet girl. On arrival, the children's hair is cut short. 'Sissy' strokes the fluffy pile of red curls that is robbed from her. Their clothes are cooked in a mighty cauldron while the tired little bodies soak in smaller disinfection baths. After a thorough towel dry, a guard distributes DDT onto their heads to prevent head lice from breeding. Freshly clothed, nauseous from the insecticide and utterly exhausted, the children creep into their bunk beds.

Sissy feels warm and safe. She no longer has to take care of her screaming little sister. Bombs seem far away.

There is only a little jet black lump of coal in her chest, a longing for her father, for the scent of cigarettes and machine oil. She closes her eyes and tries hard to imagine being scooped up in his big arms. It doesn't work, she is too tired. A young Nazi nurse with her hair combed straight back and a shiny broach on her starched collar wishes everyone a quick 'Heil Hitler', then she switches off the light. Heil Hitler? Heal Hitler? Was he sick??

It is hard for Sissy to get used to the strict camp rules. She has been a feral child, she cannot join in with the other girls, who play with dollies, made from rags. She cannot embroider and she refuses to learn. She hates sitting in long rows with others, spooning turnip soup from tin cans. Her father is gone, her sister is gone, her brothers are gone. Well, at least her mother is gone, too.

The children are constantly on the move. They head East across Germany, from the Dutch border to Bayreuth (where Saskia is astonished by the beauty of mosaics in the Eremitage) and beyond. They use trains, lorries, more often than not they walk. To begin with, the pack consists of 200 children, but more and more are left behind. Some are taken into hospitals, the lucky ones are reunited with their parents.

Onwards and onwards, off you go, children, no dawdling. Warm meals are served by Red Cross nurses in bullet riddled train stations, no one knows the destination. Wherever possible, lessons are held. If the pack stays in one place long enough, the children are sent to school. En route they are sometimes joined by teachers. It is noted that the little red head can read and write very well. Lessons may be in German here, but the letters stay the same.

The seven year old is becoming increasingly confused. The Germans took her mother, they took her Dutch father, who is now German as well, as are her brothers. The German nurses are easily identified as the enemy, they make and reinforce silly rules. But what about the machine guns?

When the children move towards Thüringen on a train full of German soldiers, stories are told, songs are sung. Little Saskia sits on the lap of a middle aged man and joins in the singing when the train comes to an abrupt halt. The laughter stops, above them the muffled roar of engines. Someone bellows an order, everyone jumps to the doors. The train bursts at its seams and spills the frightened cargo from its guts, men, children, women run in equal panic across the tracks, between wagons, towards a small hut. Whoever doesn't fit, cowers near the walls, some children place the lids of metal trash cans on their heads. Three planes dive over their heads, then the bullets come. Saskia is still out in the open, so a soldier pushes her into a ditch, throws himself over her. Then there is silence. The children look up. In the sky one of the planes has caught fire, black smoke leaks from of its tail. The children and soldiers are cheering. With a mighty crash the plane explodes somewhere in the distance.

Saskia wipes a few clumps of earth from her face and presses her lips together. She knows that in that metal case, right now, a man burns to death, another Englishman. She really wishes they would stop trying to save her.

During the day she refuses to eat the enemy's food. At night she climbs out of the window at the back, she steals turnips, carrots, sometimes an apple, and scrapes them with a piece of broken glass, her jaw is too weak to take bites. One morning, the children are lined up. One of the boys has been caught stealing a potato. The soldiers take him into the woods, the children wave him goodbye. Then they hear the short thud of a single gunshot and never see him again. Maybe the men only pretended, like the gamekeeper in Snow White? Maybe he has run away and lives with the dwarves now?

Saskia starts to eat in daylight.

Session Thirteen

Follow me now, deeper and deeper, into the pitch black of the Dipton mine in 1939.

A drift mine is a tunnel, that is hewn deep into the coal layers under the earth's surface. From the road, the main tunnel, which leads vertically down, secondary tunnels branch away into all directions. To support the ceiling, thin black columns of coal are left standing. Hewers cut the coal by hand, only rarely do they use tools operating with compressed air. Fourteen years old, Grant trades his classroom in Dipton for ten daily hours of hard physical labour in the twilight of the mines. Coal had been discovered in Dipton as early as 1333. When the reiver days were over, Armstrongs adopted mining as a way of life. Grant cannot comprehend why his ancestors decided to exchange riding the Middle Marches for an underground existence in Durham, which is, after all, on the wrong side of the Debateable lands.

Half child, half man, Grant is already too tall for the narrow shafts. But there is a war out there, so he was hired anyway. Today his cavil has decided that he and his pit mate, his marrow, will work as hand putters, pulling the full carts out, pushing empty ones back towards the hewers. At times he has to crawl on his knees and the constant bent position is such agony for him that he keeps trying to stretch, resulting in yet another bump on the head, giving his marrow a good old laugh. He could do with a steel bonnet now. His hands are full of callouses, the skin on his back torn and bloody.

Health and safety at work exists in theory only. There is a deputy who is supposed to be in charge of safety, but he is also responsible for the mine's efficiency, a deadly mix. One hundred and sixty-eight men have lost their lives in the last disaster; sixty of them were his age. He has seen the tombstones of many of his family: David Armstrong, killed by fall of stone, Daniel Armstrong, killed by explosion, ignition caused by sparks from putter picks hitting pyrites. Other memorials are reassuring, he has seen gravestones of men who died in their late sixties, still working. Never mind, there is no time for ruminations of this nature, he is paid per cart.

Despite the lack of air the pitmen often sing down here, songs were important to remain sane down here, to deal with the fear, especially after an accident. They just make them up, often on the spot, some of them are passed on. Grant particularly likes one, called The Cage.

Monday morning, Shift Number One,
Wish the day's work was over and done.
Climb in the cage, boys, let her roll!
We're the warriors who fight for the coal.
The wheels of the headgear spin around.
The cage like a stone is dropping down.
Feel the blood in your ears pound.
Down down into the ground.

First stop bottom, fall like a stone.
Halfway down lads, soon to be done.
There's a hell of a draught, a houwlin' gale,
As the cage whistles downwards, a-tellin' it's tale.

Glarin' lights, dusty floor,
Meet us there outside the cage door.
Crawl to the face, lads, sharin' a joke.
In a couple of hours you'd die for a smoke.

Sweat runs freely, matted hair,

Glistenin' bodies, black and bare.
It's damned hard work but what d'you say?
Roll on Friday when we draw our pay!

The wheels of the headgear spin around.
The cage like a stone is droppin' down.
Feel the blood in your ears pound.
Down, down into the ground.

They work in shafts too narrow for the Galloways, pit ponies, so he pulls and pushes even the heaviest loads himself. He hates this work more than anything, more than the soggy bait he has to eat in breaks that are far too short, more than the tarry oil smell and the steam. Since Jack has left he has no one to talk to anymore. His brother had become steadily weaker, one lung had been so badly affected by the coal dust that he had been transferred to the surface men. For a ten to twelve hour shift he was now paid less than before. Jack is finding it hard to bear the noise in his new found position, and the coal dust, which is shaken up in emptying the carts, does not help improve his condition.

Grant loves Jack but he cannot help see him as a weakling. Already he defeats him during their boxing matches in the forest. To make matters worse, the oldest Armstrong son has begun to perform as a Jazz musician at weekends. Last month he spent his entire wages on taking his siblings out for a day at the Whitby beach. That was no warrior. Grant swore to himself he would never end up this way.

Grant not only suffers physically from the work in the pit. Everywhere around him, out there, up there, men are fighting, and he, an Armstrong, is trapped down here like a rat in his burrow. Countless times he has attempted to volunteer, each time he has been rejected, not because he is fourteen but because he is already doing 'an irreplaceable job for England'. The mines would stand still, were all men to go to war. But he will not give up, eventually they will take him, he will manage, and angrily he pushes the cart into the twilight of the shaft.

Session Fourteen

Come back to Upper Caulfield now, to our gathering NOW.

Lothar shakes his head in disbelief. He eyed up the professor. 'It was you who left her? I thought no one ever left her?'

'I suppose I am the one exception.'

'Have you never looked back?'

'No. Never. I was glad to have her out of my life.'

'Wait a minute.' Ansgar is smiling now. 'With all due respect, that is, how did you say? A fucking load of sperm. I saw the email you sent her. That was way after she moved to Scotland, wasn't it?'

'She showed you?' The professor actually seems startled now.

'Yes, she read it to me. She was outraged. You really haven't got a clue about women, do you? Telling her you would consider taking her back. You didn't really think that would work, did you?'

'Just one second. I have just noticed something.' This voice comes from the crowd. Ferdinand, a thin tall guy steps forward. He looked as if he is intending to participate in a G8 protest march rather than attend a funeral. Leather trousers, a brown cord vest over a crinkled whitish linen shirt, Dock Martins. He is bald, except for two long braided strands of hair at the back of his head. (Daddy, you look like a bunny rabbit!)

'We have all been with her, haven't we?' Murmur of agreement in the crowd. 'Is there anyone here who hasn't, at some point, tried to get back with her?' Silence. 'Don't you think that's weird? Where are her other boyfriends, the brief little affairs, the teenage flings?'

'We were brief' call out Lothar and Erwin.

'Yes, but you tried to contact her again, didn't you?'

The two men look at each other in surprise.

'Did you?'

'Well, yes, but only once or twice. That was months after our agreement. And she had left the country by then, so it didn't really count. Did you?'

'Yes, after my wife had our youngest, I was in London at the time and I knew she lived there.'

'You had her phone number in London? How come she gave you her number?'

'Boys, boys, you're missing the point. There is something fishy about this funeral. Where are her sisters, where is her family, the kids? Where the fuck is the guy she was with last? The guy she was with when she died? And another thing – what did she die of?'

She had met Ferdinand at a film job. Her agent had asked for a family, so she had borrowed her sister's husband and child. A chance for her ex brother in law to earn that maintenance he owed her sister. It was one of the boring gigs, she could tell from the start. Candid camera. Some celebrity would find a fast food trailer in his garden and be outraged. Various 'members of the public' would walk in and order hotdogs. As usual it involved a lot of waiting and sipping coffee. The cast, a group of around twenty extras of all ages and walks of life, were waiting in a pub opposite the celebrity's garden. Anna-Ray's ex brother in law was deeply engrossed in a discussion about saxophones with a young guy in leather trousers. He looked a little unwashed and was quite apparently the exact opposite of her usual men. Although they both played the same instrument, her ex brother-in-law was a macho misogynist in a suit while the husband-to-be, at this point entirely unaware of his fate, was a deeply intellectual left wing radical. With amazingly gorgeous eyes that never once showed so much as a hint of interest in her. She tried for a few seconds to involve him in a semi-feeble attempt of a discussion about Picasso but immediately felt like a giggly little country bumpkin. So used to feigning ignorance in order to preserve masculine superiority she now felt she could not escape her act.

A few days later she saw him at another film job. This time she was dressed in a ball gown and had been given the full attention of the makeup artist. The effect was noticeable. She saw him sitting in the corner, watching her surrounded by a group of men. It was her ignorance of his very presence that drew him to her, he admitted later. They left this job together, had a meal together, spent the entire evening finding new excuses why they might as well accompany each other along the next step also. She took a train back home and he waited with her on the platform, until the moment came when they would kiss. Neither consciously liked the other at his moment but both felt as if they were still acting out another person's script. As his face approached hers she still felt uneasy, focussing too much on a small spot just under his right nostril. But then his lips touched hers and millions of little receptors in her skin triggered a tiny neuronal firework of pleasure, a chain reaction that reached both her nipples and Amygdala at the same time and entirely without warning. She never found out if he felt the same, but the fact remains that they were not parted for a single day after this moment until she pretended to see Mozart's requiem in Hamburg's St Michel four years later.

It was bliss at first, hot passion in spite of his poor personal hygiene habits. He was lovely with her son, used all the skills he had learned when working with disabled children in an earlier life. He had lived many lives. Having studied medicine until almost no aspect of love making was taboo for him. He gently lifted her onto the work surface in the kitchen and moved inside her until he came. Then he knelt down and licked her until both his and her juices mixed on the sandwich slices underneath her. When she had finished he took the bread and ate it.

After half an apprenticeship as a carpenter he had embarked on a career as a saxophonist. This would pay the rent one day. Meanwhile, he was earning his keep by erasing VHS tapes in the archive of a local television station. It came as no surprise when she discovered she was pregnant. They had planned this little adventure like a bunch of school kids planning a secret moonlight trip to a graveyard. He asked her to marry him, she declined. His mental health turned out to be too frail for the demands of a pregnancy. She was no longer lover, she was now mammal about to give birth, a mother animal.

His own mother had not given him much love. Raising concerns about young Ferdinand's clinginess at school a young teacher had informed the astonished mother that part of maternal duty was the cuddling process which, if at all possible, should be taking place on a daily basis. How long, she asked him, and, having received the necessary details, employed an egg timer to monitor the accurate administration of the prescribed warmth, holding her son on her lap for the required daily thirty minutes.

Ferdinand could not bring himself to touch the growth within her body. He distanced himself from her son. Soon, he ceased talking to her big belly, then stopped all communication, walking right through her in the flat, willing her to become a disembodied spirit in his life. At night he guarded himself against the threat of skin contact by slipping into a sleeping bag, zipped up to the chin, his head covered by a woollen hat. He used earplugs to fend off the sound waves of her sobs.

Before the baby was ready, she pushed her daughter out with the last scrapings of strength that she managed to find god knows where. For a brief moment she slipped away but she had her four year old son, and now another tiny vulnerable reason to survive, so she clawed her way back. Why did humans cast out their infants long before they were ready? These vulnerable rosy little bundles of milk scent and softness, still frail, their cells only loosely connected, ready to disintegrate at any time. It takes the glue of a parent's love to hold them together. She handed it to Ferdinand, who held his daughter and intensely looked into her face. He murmured a few words that Anna-Ray could not understand, and gently handed back the bundle. The towel was empty. Anna-Ray's head was ready to explode. How could he make a baby disappear like that? How could she just be gone? He moved into the spare room and stopped touching her. Both were dazed with the shock of their failure.

After only a few weeks, he came into her room and begged for forgiveness. He wouldn't do it again, would he? He couldn't put her through this same hell again, he simply wasn't capable of that much cruelty. And everyone deserves a second chance, her chance to find that moment she was owed, the moment in which the loving father strokes the belly of the expectant mother. That moment when he becomes excited at being kicked and starts to build a cot for the newborn. The tenderness that couples in her health advice booklets were experiencing when making love during pregnancy. Hand in hand they took a leap of faith straight into another act of procreation. They slipped and fell. The sleeping bag came back out of the cupboard and she descended into a bottomless pit. Deep in that darkness she could still taste her own pain, but she could silence herself now.

When Anna-Ray studied Japanology at the University of Hamburg she felt a leaning towards Buddhism. Zen Buddhism to be precise. Zen Koans reminded her marginally of conversations with her brother in one of his schizophrenic phases, but the concept of ending suffering by merely ending all desire made perfect sense.

Koan 68 - the Japanese emperor hears of Kakua, the first man to import Zen from China. He asks him to preach Zen for his own and his subjects' benefit. Kakua plays a single note on his flute and disappears.

Koan 69 – a cook prepares dinner for Zen master Fugai and his followers. He rushes preparations and accidentally chops off the head of a snake when cooking the vegetables. When Fugai's followers praise the soup, the master finds the snake's head in his bowl. He summons the cook. 'Oh thank you master', he says and eats the snake part quickly.

Aha. Maybe she really was just a country bumpkin, maybe he was right? The longer she lived with Ferdinand the clearer it became to her that Siddharta Gotama had behaved just like her husband. She would not end her own suffering by no longer desiring his help, his love, his support. She would alleviate his suffering.

Like the Sakya Prince he was a family father who lived more in his head than his body. Like the great teacher he would soon decide to leave his son behind and attempt to find himself. Another man who neglected his duties and escaped the rigours of family life in order to have some me-time, leaving behind a woman to stay in the here and now, consoling children, handling bills.

How did Yasudhara cope with bringing up their son Rahula once her husband had renounced all earthly goods and desires of the flesh? Who considered her desires? She had conceived her son the night Buddha fled. Was she ever touched again?

Anna-Ray learned a lot in her Zen Buddhism class. She asked Ferdinand to move out and shaved her head bald. Her son decided that she no longer needed to pick him up from primary school.

'Why is her family not here?' Ferdinand had not finished. He had had doubts about this sick little get-together from the start. It wasn't the fact that she had organised all this in advance without possibly knowing she was going to die soon. They all knew she had been suicidal, she had tried a few times in her teens, never made a secret about the fact that she found the thought of a long future horrifying. Live to my eighties, she used to say, that's another fifty odd years of breathing in, breathing out, flashbacks and fucking nightmares. But she had also said that she would never try again, for the kid's sake. Had she found a method that was foolproof, one that would not arouse the life insurer's suspicion?

But there was another thing that worried him. Why could he not remember getting here? At that point he spotted movement. Something was inside the grave. Had an animal fallen in while they had been distracted by the amusing battle between the old man and the professor? Others spotted the creature, too. No, it was not his imagination, something was alive in there and trying to get out. What the fuck was going on?

Session Fifteen

Even if we are spared destruction by war, our lives will have to change if we want to save life from self-destruction.

Aleksandr Solzhenitsyn

I am now asking you to return to Durham. It is 1944 and Grant is trying to get into the army.

'Well, boy, let's get the measure of you.' The military doctor points at the measuring level on the wall. Grant squints, over there, a long shape, could that be it? He rises and walks into the direction indicated. In front of the tape measure he attempts to hunch as much as possible. He knows he is too tall for the parachute regiment, but it's worth a shot. The doctor only briefly glances in his direction and takes a note. He nods. 'Next.'

The war has gone on for far too long, the nation's need for new cogs in the war machine is great. For the first time since his metamorphosis from miner to steelworker, the young man stands a real chance of being accepted into the army. All hail to his bruised and battered back. And, of course Jack. One took care of his release from the factory, the other got him this new job. He is lucky to find a position, the war makes anything possible.

Days later Private Armstrong holds the long desired piece of paper in his hands. 'Invictus fucking maneo', he murmurs, before he begins to pack. 'I bloody well do remain unvanquished.'

Burma cannot be described in words. How can a man talk of an experience he himself has not begun to grasp? He does not regret the killing, but he is risking his life for the wrong country. Everything he does is secret, he will never be able to tell. A poisonous little worm begins to grow in his gut; it feeds on memories so cruel that even this mountain of a man is incapable of defeating them.

It is early morning. Heavy raindrops explode on the roof of the tent, here and there a few drops make it through. Grant rolls on his side, tries desperately to shelter from the damp. It stinks to high heavens. These men have not seen a bath in months. He has to get out. Carefully he straightens up; he does not want to startle his pal. Before he slides his feet into his boots he turns them around, shakes them, until he is sure it's yellow-mamba-free. The day before yesterday one of the men fell over, silently, expressionless. They had found a tiny bite wound on his toe. And a squashed snake. Lance Corporal Armstrong pulls the zip of the tent opening down. Goddamn jungle. A piercing scream behind him makes him jump aside. Japs? No, it's his tent buddy, racing past him into the bush like a maniac, hands pressed onto his face. By the time they catch up with him he is rolling around on the earth, moaning. His face has been erased beyond recognition. The second case this week. 'What is this, what the fuck did this?' A young Indian points at the tent. He gesticulates, arms flailing, until one of their Ghurkha trainers translates: 'It was monkey urine.' Monkey piss. One of the fucking little shites has pissed onto the tent. God help us, in this fucking country even the fucking monkeys piss acid. Whatever next?

Grant is trained in Chinese, Urdu and Japanese. He even learns to imitate animal noises. Only with time he begins to suspect they will deliver him straight to the mouth of hell – Special Air Service. Members of this unit are trained to kill so efficiently they will be afraid for the rest of their lives that they may kill a member of their own family in a rash instinctive startle response. This unit has not been in existence long, they do not even have their own badge yet. Grant knows he will be required to erase his time here both in his memory and in his conscience.

None of the men are prepared when the call comes in April. They are the Durham Light Infantry, part of the British second division, huddled together in a small plane.

To the brave of both nations
Flodden Field, British Borders 1513
Kohima, Burma 1944
Lock the door, Lariston, lion of Liddesdale

Lock the door, Lariston, Lowther comes on

The Armstrongs are flying, the widows are crying

Castletown is burning and Oliver is gone.

James Hogg

Have you ever entered a chicken coop after the fox has paid a visit? It's as if something has exploded, not quite a two-inch mortar, a light machine gun maybe, aided by a machete, possibly a grenade, insufficient to blow the structure itself up, enough impact for you to find bits of chicken everywhere, splattered across the straw, stuck to the ceiling. You will not find a single chicken left alive, whether there were two, three or twenty to begin with. The fox does not need to kill them all, he will not be able to eat anywhere near as many. If he were able to reason he would understand that his chances of getting caught increase exponentially with the length of time spent killing. But then, he is not able to reason. After that first bite the fox loses control, his jaw muscles become tense, his only focus is to tear and shred. The killing frenzy will not stop until the predator has eliminated all prey. In nature the chicken would have a chance to run, but here they are trapped.

In 1944, 100,000 Japanese troops march towards Imphal and Kohima. They are to seize the two British bastions in Northern Burma before cutting off the Bengal-Assam railway 30 miles north. They are confident that the Amritsa-bred hatred of the British is big enough to support a Japanese advance into India. Of the 100,000 proud Japanese cockerels, only 50,000 will find their way out of the Kohima coop, perched 5,000 feet high on a saddle in the Naga hills.

What do the foxes feel before they are dropped out of the plane? What does Grant feel when he fires that first shot, slashes his machete into another man's skin for the first time? Does it get stuck in the bone? Is it difficult to penetrate the thick canvas of his jacket, or his collar? How does it feel a second time, a third, a fourth, a fifth? At what point do his jaw muscles become tense? Lying shoulder to shoulder with his mates, how close do the Japanese spring grenades come? When the body goes into fight or flight, it is flooded with adrenaline. The heart pumps faster to carry extra strength into the muscles. The blood is taken away from other areas in the body, less important ones, such as the brain and stomach. Nausea sets in, a feeling of light headedness, tunnel vision. The body needs to cool down, sweat pours, dehydrating the predator. More calories are burned than during a half marathon, the body needs calories. Have they brought provisions or do they take the dead man's ball of rice, his dried fish?

On Flooden Field King James IV of Scotland prepares for an invasion of England. After a welcome but brief distraction by Lady Heron, he proceeds to Durham Cathedral, collecting the sacred banner of St Cuthbert. He prays for victory.

With him ride the Border reivers. They wear the simple back and breast armour of a pike man, their heads protected by steel bonnets. Their eighteen foot pikes look menacing but the men know they are useless without clear formation.

Grant arrives when Montagu Stopford's 33rd Corps is losing hope, isolated on the hilltop they are encircled by the Japanese, defending inch by inch by the skin of their teeth. Not long and the trees are carpeted with parachutes, the ruins are covered in dead bodies. Against all odds, the 1st Royal Berkshires and the 2nd Durham Light Infantry hold Garrison Hill.

James orders the burning of a camp defuse. Under cover of the thick wall of smoke James moves the entire Scottish army on top of Branxton hill. From here they wait for the English.

An ammunition dump is hit, the shadows of the Japanese infantry against the wall of smoke gives their location away.

In the end it's a tennis court that separates the Japanese from the British and Indian troops. Thanks to a District Commissioner's decadence a Lee tank finds open battle space. The Japanese withdraw, leaving bodies, shells and swords behind.

The Scottish Borderers, led by Lord Home, charge downhill, frightening Edmund's men into escape. The braver chickens remain and face swift slaughter. King James' jaw tenses, he rides into the onslaught, and with him dies the battle. The English win.

The Borderers collect the weapons of the slain along with anything else shiny, the British bring home Samurai swords.

> We'll here nae mair lilting at our ewe milking,
> Women and bairns are heartless and wae,
> Sighing and moaning on a ilka green loaning,
> The flowers of the forest are wede away.

From April onwards the men are to comb the jungle individually, cutting off enemy supplies – and in the course of this cut off their heads and collect Jap ears on their belts. Their return is not mentioned, not many will make it.

Grant's men desperately fight a Japanese patrol unit. No guns stand between their conscience and the kill, the echo of the shots would attract the enemy. The young Brit loses feeling in his right arm, he uses his machete like a butcher's knife. Soldiers call this method of killing a Hulu bash, it's the most common method in the East. Grant receives his wages from the Indian army, he has lost all count of who he has come here to fight for. The uniforms are so muddy it is hard to tell who is friend, who is foe. Everyone's skin is brown. Europe is one big post war celebration, here Ghurkha, Brits, Aussis, Kiwis, Indian men fight tooth and nail against the nameless leftovers of the Emperor's mighty army, that refuse to back down.

It is 1948. A corporal sits on the stairs of a hotel. He is surrounded by natives, proudly shows photos of terrorists that have been killed by the British troops. The army had nailed corpses to the back of the vans and trailed them through the Kampongs from which they had drafted their recruits.

When an enemy soldier, or someone who is mistaken for one at the time, is killed, his ear or hand is cut off and collected on the victor's belt, a gruesome trophy of skill over conscience. Brits and Ghurkhas equally have sworn never to return an unbloodied machete into its sheath. If a soldier has not killed, he will cut his own hand at the end of the day. Grant has one scar on his stomach, his hands are without blemish.

Session Sixteen

It is 1945 and the war is over. We need to rush to Germany and see how Saskia is doing. At first it is only rumours, whispers, another fairytale. But then they come – the English soldiers are here, they are real. Saskia decides she likes the British very much.

Together with the English and the Americans come the Russians. People run away in panic, countless lines of lorries pass the astonished kids.

An American soldier with black skin approaches her. She is puzzled. She wants to touch him, find out if there would be stains on her hand. He takes out a tiny parcel, no bigger than a matchbox, and hands it to her. He nods to her as if to encourage her. She is not sure what to do. He mimics eating, moving his hand to his mouth, making chewing and swallowing noises, then he lets out a long yummmmmmmmm sound and rubs his enormous stomach. She smells the packet, it is delicious. She opens it, carefully peeling the paper back, first the outside, then the shiny metal paper inside. She finds a disappointingly greyish brown hard substance. Still keeping one eye on the soldier she lifts the stuff and sniffs again. Saliva accumulates in her mouth. She takes a nibble, a tiny bit at first, then more. Smell and taste mix in her mouth, play with the receptors on her tongue, laugh and giggle all the way into her brain and back down her spine, deep into her stomach. This is too much pleasure. She closes her eyes and concentrates on the lingering taste sensation. When she opens them again the man has left. Had he given her a piece of his skin? Or had he simply covered himself in this delicious stuff. Whatever it was, she wants more.

Don't look so confused. I know it is not what you observed when you were watching her. This is the story she will tell her children. It's a great story. Much better than saying that she missed most of the liberation, she was ill with dysentery. Everyone else seemed to have adorable Negro stories, they were always tall and broad shouldered with a friendly grin. She knows what chocolate is, she used to steal it from her father's pocket when he deliberately looked away. But they do hand out chewing gum, and tangerines.

The children's march is not over. They are taken to an old abandoned castle in Lüchow-Dannenberg, where a provisional camp is built for them. The pack feels safe and confused.

Shortly after they are joined by another group of children. Among the little ones a blonde girl named Annegret Puschat. 'Here is your sister, can you believe it?' the Red Cross nurse asks her. Well, yes, she can, but she does not know how to feel about it. The girls do not recognize each other, they have grown to be strangers. Time in the castle passes comfortably. No more fear of bombings, there is even enough to eat. One afternoon, Saskia is permitted to collect frozen sloe berries. On her return she is greeted by one of the nurses: 'Sissy, Sissy, look what a present we have for you!' 'Papa!' And there he is. Still in uniform, his bag shouldered, his arms wide open. He used the Red Cross to find out where his daughter is and has come to collect her. What a surprise when he finds out his little one is here also.

In January, the children are lifted onto a goods wagon, atop tree trunks, wrapped in frozen rain, they head into the night. A woman is trying desperately not to slip off the perilous ice and their father pulls her over. He asks her to warm his girls with her body and covers them with a smelly old tarpaulin. He will not lose them to one lousy winter's night.

The woman enquires through clenched teeth where they are headed. 'First to Wuppertal, to my father, then Holland, maybe Leeuwarden.' Once again, Karma winks at them with a smirk, the thankful lady is married to a border guard, who will later help smuggle the family into the Netherlands. For now though they stay with granddad Puschat, a straight backed man who, in the confusion of war, had ensured not only his own survival by collecting wood and acorns. Heinrich finds out that his son Georg is alive, he was placed as a farm hand in Aachen. Anni is left with granddad, Saskia and her father leave immediately to collect him. He is in reasonable health and ready to brave the journey across the border, in the dark of the night, illegally, aided by their newfound ally. Malnourished little Saskia fits in her father's military bag. They cross meadows, climb under barbed wire, dodge spotlights. Now, finally, they are home.

But the journey is far from over. They are passed from relative to relative, a brief reunion with her mother leaves Saskia disappointed. Frouwkje has started a new life, she has opened a hostel with a friend and enjoys her childless life. Saskia has never really missed her, but she was hoping she might find her brother Leo with her.

When the skeleton of Leo is finally released from its Russian prison, his bones rattle with dysentery, typhoid and nightmares. He had been a pretty young boy when he left, enemy of the Reich, Dutch 'volunteer', servicing the soldiers of the German Waffen SS, who were lonely and frustrated at the Russian front, looking for entertainment in the absence of their Frauleins. Only the Russians had acknowledged he was Dutch and released him early. He had not been eating turnips.

Heinrich allows his son to have two spoons of soup, then he calls the doctor.

Life returns to normal. Saskia is sent to school, Heinrich meets Mevrouw Tels, a good looking Jewish woman, whose marriage had also fallen casualty to the war. Joined by her two sons, they return to Amsterdam. Leo finds work at a brewery, Georg begins an apprenticeship in the iron industry. Saskia does what she loves best, she roams the city. In good weather she jumps onto her slightly defective bike, in bad weather she jumps onto the tram. The young woman lives in a feeling of eternal bliss. She does well at school, her father is creative again, he makes signs. In other words, the war is behind them. She thinks. One evening, another knock on the door teaches her otherwise, it's the military police. 'Child', her father whispers, 'we have to leave.' Saskia packs everything she can get her hands on into a yellow wicker basket with brown handles. At the door the policeman takes it off her. 'Only the clothes on your body.' Even Anni, who has been staying with her grandmother for recovery, is collected and thrown into prison with the rest. At this point Heinrich loses his temper. Beside himself he kicks the cell door, he shouts he cries. 'Why the baby, she is a toddler, you cannot lock her up. You will regret this, I have never done anything to harm my country, I am Dutch, godverdomme!'

Three months it takes before they hear the call: 'Tomorrow assemble in the court yard for transport, transport to Germany.'

Session Seventeen

We are back at Upper Caulfield. It is NOW and yet another lover demands attention.

"I guess it's time for me to speak". The young man is in his twenties, he looks like Adrian Brody and David Schwimmer's secret love child. How can he be so young? They all know who he is, he had visited her throughout her life, they had met when she was sixteen, parted on friendly terms when she was eighteen and remained friends since. His name was Burkhard. That was over twenty-three years ago. How could he be so young? Did he have surgery? Was there a picture in someone's attic?

"I missed a lot about her. I tried to pay attention but I still missed a lot. I still miss a lot of her." A short speech but to the point. No one is listening anyway. Everyone is now transfixed by the scurrying and shuffling in the grave. That is no small animal.

They had met at a café near Hanover. Anna-Ray had just finished with her boyfriend and had spent the day in sloppy clothes and no makeup, roaming around town treating herself. If something bad happened she always felt she needed a treat, just to even things out. She bumped into them outside the cinema, her best buddy Walter and a stranger. Tall, handsome, young, black eyes glowing over a nose of promising proportions. An der Nase eines Mannes erkennt man seinen Johannes... you measure a man's willie by the size of his nose. Why did the Germans call it a John and the English a Willie? In fact the English used a Johnnie to cover their willies, she had sniggered.

They had hot chocolate together and she dropped a biscuit in his cup, laughing (she is funny, one point for her). He was intrigued and missed the point completely. She was testing him. Would he get angry? The next day they went out together and she scrubbed up so well that he was hooked (that's got to be worth two points). He arrived late (first minus point noted) and tried to play it cool by not paying her a compliment (second minus point). By the time they arrived at the restaurant he was another five points down for taking pictures of ancient doorknobs, cracks in the pavement and several interesting houses but none of her.

'Where did you go?'

'A steak house. We always went to a steak house.'

At the entrance he opened the door for her (a point earned) and she accepted without so much of a hint of women's lib sarcasm (another two for her). He lost another three points by being difficult and choosy with the waitress, she earned some more by not smoking and ordering a non-alcoholic drink. The evening progressed well after that. They had a lovely conversation and the food was good. They discovered that they were both cineholics. She looked at him, he looked at her. He had such nice eyes, she had such sensuous lips, he was leaning towards her, he really did have large nostrils, filled with hair, was that a tiny white piece of bogey waving her away from his face?

He was talking about the latest Jim Jarmusch. Such a brilliant director. Had she seen the part where they met in the prison cell? 'I screama you screama we all screama for ice screama' Hilarious. Good, the little slimy thing was gone. Did that mean he wiped it off with his hand? What if he tried to take hers now? She lost count.

They did end up kissing, days later, in his flat. She was still wearing the work outfit from her Sunday job at the café, white blouse, tight black skirt, little white apron.

Within minutes they were approaching intimacy and he felt it was time to explain his three towel rule.

'The three towel rule, I know that one.'

'Yeah, so do I. That was you?'

'What's the three towel rule?'

'You don't know that one? He explained to her that she could stay in his flat after but that, if she wanted to take a shower in the morning, she should use the three towels in the bathroom in a particular order. Maybe you should explain that one yourself?'

'I haven't got a clue what you are talking about.'

'The big one was for the head, wasn't it, and the small one for the arms or something.'

'No, the big one is for the waist and the two smaller ones are for the face and hair if you must know.'

'Ah, so the three towel rule does exist? And you tried to get Anna-Ray to follow it? Is that why she left you in the end?'

'She didn't leave me. We parted ways in mutual agreement and a very pleasant last kiss after two years of splitting up on a regular basis.'

'Have you ever regretted it?'

'Why are you asking me that? Who are you anyway?'

He cannot remember saying any of this out loud, but they had obviously heard his story. Oh god, is that Walter over there in the wheelchair? He feels sick. Walter can not be here, he died three years ago, drowned by the fluid in his lungs. He remembers their last visit in his house. Anna-Ray had asked him to accompany her. Walter had been lying in his bed in the living room, red with fever. He had been joking, seductively removing the bed cover from his support-stockinged legs ('Look, I put these on specially for you, darling.') but his eyes had been wide with fear.

But there he is, a little younger even than he remembers him. And behind him, that male nurse, is that Sigmund? Her lover when she was sixteen? He has to be Sigmund's son, surely, he looks about seventeen now. What is happening? He looks around him, half expecting to find cameras. And then it hits him. He pulls a small mirror out of his coat pocket and slowly raises it to his face. His lines are gone. His twelve o'clock shadow is darker than ever, none of the salt and pepper dots he has grown to accept. His hair is completely black. His stomach churns, his head begins to spin. Is he going to pass out? He places his right middle finger onto his artery, thank god, his heart is still beating, but is that a lump? Maybe he has eaten something bad? How ridiculous. There is a fever, surely, maybe he was having a stroke? Has he packed the right pills for this? Maybe he could have a brief glimpse in his medical book and check? For a brief moment he loses his balance and stumbles towards the hole but instinct pulls him back immediately.

He can see the reason why everyone around him has grown silent.

A hand stretches out of the grave, dirty fingernails, earth in the finest cracks of its skin, clawing at the loose sidewall, searching to gain hold. A strong hand, pale skin, hairy, a man's hand, the fingertips stained dark yellow. He feels the urge to vomit and run away simultaneously but remains glued to the spot. He is no longer here of his own free will, he understands that. Are they even here to bury her? Or have they been summoned to uncover something? Has this thing, this man, been down there all this time or did he slip in while they were digging? Was this what she wanted them to see? He shivers. He makes no attempt to move closer to the hole, he already knows who this is. They all know.

Session Eighteen

Things are getting a little intense. You are exhausted and confused. I understand. Take a small break and come to this safe place. You are in Germany, it is 1988. This is Anna-Ray's short story.

'Is Julien in?' 'Yes, wait, I will get you the key.'

Laya's bistro is bursting at the seams, as usual around this time. Where else are you meant to go in this godforsaken German town? The young girl squeezes through two British soldiers, stretches her arm across the bar. One of the boys cannot resist temptation.

'Hi gorgeous, have a seat.'

'2-8-2', she recites quietly and slowly, holding eye contact. He freezes and withdraws his tattooed hand from her hip. His attention focuses firmly on his beer. Nothing works as quickly as the number of the military police. They often have trouble with Squaddies around here. Victors, occupiers, peacekeepers, although more often than not it is clear that no peace contract has been signed. A boy in her class crossed a bridge at the wrong time. He was beaten by three drunken soldiers, who discarded his body into the river. He managed to swim ashore with four broken ribs.

"Out of Bounds" is a common sign at bar doors these days. Dutch soldiers, Americans, they're all fine, but Squaddies spell trouble. It is not uncommon to see a young soldier burn his arm with a cigarette butt, just to feel something. These are the men she has to walk past on her way to school; they are standing in front of the NAAFI, armed with machine guns. No one knows they are not loaded. British dependants use that shop, women walk in with their hair still in curlers, children are never dressed for the cold German weather, often running around in shorts and T-Shirts, clutching a pack of salt and vinegar, when German kids grab their skates and go for a glide on the frozen river. She wonders if all British are like that.

The metal door to the flat above the bistro is jammed, it needs a little persuasion before it releases her from the smoke filled room into a hybrid larder/staircase. She enjoys the privilege of being permitted into the hallowed rooms of the owner. The walls lining the staircase are filled with black and white snaps of exotic and childlike women. She herself is only seventeen, with the typical round features and full lips of an accomplished Lolita, but she is not one of them. He truly does love her.

Her unpractised ankles struggle to climb the heavily carpeted stairs in high heels. The ancient buildings in the centre of the small German town are as narrow as the minds of its citizens – and laugh in the face of any spirit level. She has arrived in front of his door and hesitates. Does she smell good? Is her lipstick red enough? The hem of her skirt has moved up, allows a peek of the lace top of her silk stockings.

Perfect. The carefully created vamp attire shelters her racing heart.

Julien is not just any man. The owner of the trendiest place in town, photographer and artist. He has designed all items of furniture in the Bistro himself – he even built them. He is surrounded by an aura of Big City intellect and existentially black turtlenecks. She knocks a little too quietly. Oh well, at least she had instructed her mother to pretend she wasn't in for the last four days. This kind of thing makes a woman interesting to a man. On the table a half empty bottle of red, two dried up glasses, one of them marked with lipstick. An overfilled ashtray. He doesn't smoke.

He looks sheepish. 'Let me explain', he blurts out and suddenly she is so much older than he. 'You weren't there when I needed you.' With calculated dispassion she settles on one of his self-made chairs, she owns this moment. Damn these chairs are uncomfortable, why has she never noticed that before? The silk of her stockings rustles softly as she places one leg over the other. Julien rambles of loneliness and the sad looking woman from his past, who needed to hear that he no longer loved her. He talks of her collapse, unbearable for him. Anna-Ray cannot help but admire her adversary's skill. Neediness as opposed to independence, clever, if supported by the appropriate amount of tears – enough to slightly smudge mascara, increasing the come hither and rescue me effect, not so much that snot streams out of a reddened and swollen nose. And cigarettes, so lazy and oral, whoever she was, she was good. The poor man had no idea he was a pawn, expecting to control a game of chess. As if by chance, the lapel of her blazer reveals the small birthmark, and a hint of breast silences him. The phone rings. He picks up the receiver. 'Not now…bad timing…maybe…later…okay, I will see you in a minute.' He puts the phone down, looks at her with that wet wipe expression. 'I don't know why I have just done that.'

'You go ahead.' She takes the wine bottle and rests the opening just above her lower lip. A small trickle of red liquid glides down her chin, along her slender neck, into her cleavage. His eyes follow and he kneels in front of her. A button, another one, the wine flows and is caught with his tongue. This time he forgets his trademark candles and old Aznavour vinyls.

Sometime around 5 am she is wakened by the noise of the market vendors opening their stalls. Cool morning air sleepily mingles with sweat and dawn. On her chest the dried remains of wine and sperm. She searches for her clothes, strewn across the floor. One stocking remains hidden. Then she sneaks down the creaky stairs into that twilight zone outside, somewhere between darkness and day. On the market square someone throws her a golden delicious. She smiles and throws back her rolled up second stocking. One ravenous bite of apple chases away the stale taste of the previous night.

Anna-Ray wrote this story when she was eighteen. She had walked into Julien's bedroom, found the bottle and ashtray, had burst into tears and ran away, all snot and swollen eyelids, then she banned the event into her notebook and gave it a different ending. See, isn't that better? Are you relaxed again?

Session Nineteen

Look up to the right corner of your eye. Now to the middle. Now to the left corner. Deep breath. And return to Germany, in the winter of 1946.

One hundred and sixty people are loaded into trucks, efficiently and well organised. Every second lorry is followed by a policeman on motorcycle. When they pass the town boundaries, someone starts to sing 'Muss I denn muss I denn zum Städtele hinaus, Städtele hinaus, aber du mein Schatz bleibst hier..' and the others join in.

The journey ends in camp Lüstringen, near Osnabrück, a temporary camp for refugees. Compared to the impoverished refugees from the East the Puschats look like royalty, but a daily diet of cabbage soup and damp tents are an efficient equaliser. Heinrich finds out who denounced him to the Germans when the war began. He escapes from the camp, crosses the border and lets out all his anger on the little village policeman from Epe. When he leaves the bloody body he does not know if he has killed him.

He acquires food and medicine at his mother's, then he returns to the border and turns himself in. He is taken back to the camp where his children await him, sick with fear. Leo works in a sugar cane factory, he steals canes, which, boiled and dried on a washing line, can be traded as sweets. Potatoes are stolen from the fields of nearby farmers. Cut into wafer thin slices and cooked against the metal of a provisional stove they become deliciously decadent crisps.

At Christmas, her father has the ingenious idea of cutting out stars, bells and other shapes from cardboard. Dunked in glue and sprinkled with grated metal they make beautiful tree decorations. Little Saskia sells them for ten Pfennig a piece. With her wide brown eyes and her cute Dutch accent she has no problems selling out. Occasionally, the soldiers throw away cigarette butts, Saskia collects them, her dad smokes them in his silver cigarette tip, the one item he has refused to pawn.

Finally, Heinrich's begging letters to the Dutch government have led to partial success: The girls, only the girls, are allowed to return to the Netherlands, provided they can stay with a relative. Anni and Saskia are collected by two Dutch policemen, fed white bread and kept in a Dutch camp for fourteen days. Nobody comes to collect them. When they are finally returned to the camp in Lüstringen their father's face turns white with rage.

They are obviously unwanted in their homeland. Heinrich makes up his mind. He tells the children that Hitler was pelted with rotten eggs when he marched into Wuppertal, so this is where they will live from now on, and that's an end to that.

How do you explain to a child the story of a communist worker's union that organised a resistance to the Nazi regime? A resistance resulting in the arrest and mass trials of more than 1900 German workers. Let's call it egg throwing. In any case this city will be more accepting of those who resisted and collaborated.

Session Twenty

You are back in England. It is 1960. The sun stands red above the hills of Dipton. Music travels from the distant Armstrong house, where Grant is getting ready for the annual summer festival. A parachute jump gone wrong has left its signature on his forehead: a bright red line runs across as if his brain has been removed. A receding hairline is no longer covering it. Should he wear a hat?

On one of the benches he spots the very woman he came here to meet. An elegant dress emphasises hidden curves, tasteful accessories betray a hint of city. He had watched her yesterday in Gateshead, but greasy and covered in muck from working on his car he had thought it wiser to wait. Now, however, he is ready. 'Good evening. May I join you?' She lifts an eyebrow. A local boy, his accent gives him away. She cannot help but stare at his forehead. 'What is this? She blurts out? 'An accident?' 'No, it happened in Burma.' Immediately she slides aside, frees a space for him.

'Please, have a seat. I am Gladys.' 'Grant, pleased to meet you.'

They are married the same year in the same chapel where Grant was baptised. His brother Jack cannot attend, he has succumbed to the cancer which the coal dust had nourished in his lungs. Tiny now lives in an asylum for the mentally insane. Mary was married before him but her husband, too, has passed away, in a traffic accident. She brings her son Michael.

The young couple buy a house on Dipton's main street. Grant settles for a life without war, he even starts his own vegetable garden. He ignores his mother in law, who insists her daughter has married beneath her circumstances.

One year later Grant finds himself sitting on the empty frame of his marital bed, the only piece of furniture left behind by Gladys. A fast end to a fast paced marriage. He betrayed her, she betrayed him. He threw her out, she left. Where now? He stares at the phone. It is still connected.

<u>His</u> indiscretions were committed with a married German woman, who was as sick of this country as she was of her British husband. She has asked Grant to run away with her, to her native city, Lübeck. A sigh, a shrug, then he picks up the receiver and begins to dial.

Session Twenty-One

Take a look at this:

Federal Republic of Germany, Lübeck, 28 September 1965

Dear Mary and Michael,

Just a few lines thanking you for your letter and papers.

The weather has been warm and sunny but now it has changed to wind and rain. I have been working anytime lately and going to work on Saturdays till 4- all I seem to be doing is working. I am in first shift this week 6 till 5 but it gets dark soon and I can only work in the garden on Sundays.

I am sending some more transfers for Michael's car. They cost almost 3 ½ d each so if he wants any more let me know.

Well, Tiny wrote today but she thinks I should write everyday but what is there to write about.

I am in perfectly good health have a good lodge plenty to eat and a good job so what more can I ask for. There is nothing so ever to worry about. I am now beginning to speak and write more German in fact everyone at work thinks I am German. Another year here and I will be doing alright much more than In England.

Next month I go back to school night classes ABEND KURSE FÜR AUSLÄNDER. I have to go tomorrow see about it.

Well as I say there isn't a great deal to write about.

All my love
Bruder Grant

Grant lives in Lübeck. His affair with the married woman resulted in a daughter. He has not been able to cope and has left them. She decided to return to her husband, who has accepted the girl as his own. It's better for the bairn. There is no garden, he speaks hardly any German and will never fully master this language. His sister Tiny has never left the hospital for the clinically insane.

Session Twenty-Two

You are still relaxed. You have returned to check up on Saskia, who now lives in Wuppertal, in Germany. The country is still licking the bruises and cuts of its self inflictied war wounds. When the children of the war return to school, they are not easily tamed. What can a teacher threaten them with that they haven't already survived? After only one day Saskia decides she will not go back. The other children, obviously no cleverer than her, laugh at her 'cute' accent and her flaming red curls. She persistently emphasises the wrong syllable, even the teacher grins. For weeks she fakes attendance while running around the streets of Wuppertal until she is finally caught by a social worker. In order to make her reintegration easier she is sent to a girl's home, not a smart move. The insolent twelve year old tries everything to be sent back home. She disturbs the other children's nap, she climbs trees, she listens to no one. When even kitchen duty shows no effect, Saskia wins, she is allowed to return to Wuppertal.

Everything is changed. A stranger picks her up from the station and introduces herself as her stepmother's niece. Stepmother? It's true, her father lives with a new woman, Elfriede Füllbeck, she works in the local textile factory. The new house resembles a dove cote. Once sheltered by neighbouring buildings it has been orphaned in the bombings, its back wall reaches aimlessly into the sky. They keep a horse in the cellar, at night it shuffles and stomps. During the day it has to pull a cart of coal.

Saskia does not get on well with 'Friedchen', as her dad calls her affectionately. This woman has no style whatsoever! If she lays the table with forks only, Saskia gets the napkins and knives. Friedchen considers unnecessary luxuries a sin. Saskia considers them a reason to live, a means for survival. She picks flowers and places them in the centre of the table. 'Sissy, Sissy', Friedchen moans, 'What is to become of this child!'

When Saskia decides to attend school, Friedchen charges her for her sandwich. Then she charges her for the paper it is wrapped in.

Wuppertal is still lying in ruins. Teenagers enjoy climbing the highest walls and rummage in the deepest most disgusting cellars, Saskia is among them. They steal from the backyard of a metal scrap merchant and sell the goods back to him at the front door. They take fruit if they want it and pick flowers in abandoned gardens.

Leo works in scrap metal, Georg helps rebuild the roads, Heinrich is self employed. He trades in textiles, so their little home is overrun with boxes, cartons, lengths of fabric. Shelves are always full and people buy.

Against all odds Saskia has managed to gain her school qualifications without effort. Now she is expected to learn a decent trade. She would prefer something else – her heart is set to work with food. Work in a restaurant – access to meat, vegetables, salads. Work in a café – access to pastries, desserts, cream cakes. Despite her stepmother's objections she attempts to gain employment in this area until, after a long fight, Heinrich forbids her to continue.

Saskia applies for a job as a stewardess, she is accepted, all she needs now is the money to complete a six week training, for this she would have to rely on her parents' support. In the 50s it is not possible for a woman to move into another city without financial backup. Predictably, her parents refuse.

After a time spent in desperate frustration her father decides she is destined for a career in sales, like him. She starts her new life in a small coffee shop and does very well to begin with. She is pleasant and easy on the eye, but it is not long before her rebellious character breaks through the icing.

Saskia is instructed to spend her entire afternoon breaking nuts with a kilo weight, then fill the splinters into 100g bags. The kilo weight is heavy so she shows initiative and brings in her own nutcracker. Management is appalled. You have been told to use the weight; you will use the weight, young lady. Either you will do as you are told or you should look for another job. Saskia agrees. She does not return.

In the family she becomes known as the child that causes difficulty, oh well, after all she has been through, no wonder. She is given another chance.

There is a street in Wuppertal, called Hofaue. This street has come to fame as one of the most prestigious textile production places in Europe. It is the home of tanneries, dye works, weavers, spinning mills, embroidery, industrial sewing, corporate wear and designer fabrics. In the mornings crowds of workers stream into the street, pushing along the pavement before they filter into the many different entrances. Saskia is accepted as seamstress and joins the movement of the masses. The little factory, run by Mr and Mrs Hannes, produces beautiful garments, mainly silken nightwear. Whatever is made here needs to be flawless. Saskia manages to fit in for three years. She attends college once a week and surprises herself more than anyone by completing her apprenticeship. Her theory exam is good, her practical average. She has attached a silken pocket three and a half millimetres too high, otherwise she would have done fine, she tells her parents with a quivering lip.

Once she has completed her apprenticeship Saskia feels as if she has come round from a very long coma. She hates this job. All this regularity, all this order, the monotony. The only thing keeping her from insanity is her friend Eva, or more precisely, Eva's job as a costume maker, which enables her to smuggle anyone into the opera for free. The girls choose the most expensive seats in the house, these are the ones hardly every taken. They are not choosy, operas, musicals, as long as they get to wear the latest fashion, Pepita dresses, collars with giant cherry patterns, high heels.

But something is missing with the outfit, Sissy finds out. She decides it's a black shirt, yellow tie and black tight jeans – including content - a young man called Günther. He looks lovely, has arrived here from Sweden and tops any other man when it comes to style. His brylcreemed hair is combed to form a ducks arse in the back of his head, so smart, so manly, and seven years older than her. Saskia smells freedom on him, liberation from floor wax, boredom, orderliness and checking door frames for dust ; she will have a home, her own home, no more moving around. To begin with, they will have to live in a small holding camp in Lübeck, where Günther has been promised a flat, a brand new one, it has not even been built yet.

An engagement party is not permitted, so Günther hands his fiancée a ring in the street, the couple have a quick glass of wine, then he leaves to make preparations. Three months later she follows him. Her future husband collects her at the train station, he holds a giant bunch of flowers. The young bride to be looks enchanting, she wears a tiny pink suit, matching handbag, white gloves and a glorious white hat. When Günther takes her in his arms she makes a shocking discovery: she feels nothing for him.

Session Twenty-Three

I have a treat for you now. Close your eyes and listen – you can hear the voice of Saskia herself. This is what she said when her daughter interviewed her in Germany in 1995:

'After a few months everything was prepared and Günther and I were permitted to marry. No one from Wuppertal came to give me away, there was not one member of my family. I stood between strangers and it felt like a nightmare. But then so did the marriage. I became pregnant almost exactly one year later, and then I had Schorsch. While I was in hospital the flat was finished. On the outside everything seemed to be on the up. You have no idea what conditions in the holding camp were like!'

'Hang on, Mama, I spoke with the others, we agreed that the time with the other husbands should maybe be left out.'

'Well, ok, but then you still have to mention that I was divorced in the end'

'And that you married again and were divorced again, so that you ended up with four children.' Two from the first, two from the second.'

'Oh god, when you put it that way, you are maybe best to leave that out as well. Or just briefly touch on it. Maybe you could say two more marriages ended in divorce. Whichever language you use, it was a turbulent time. But however they ended, they were marriages that I entered lovingly end ended badly, due to circumstances. It is merely a fact that I was left behind again, dealing with things on my own. But then, you know all about that yourself, don't you? You were divorced and have been a single mum longer than I ever was.'

Lübeck, Germany, 1968

Grant sits on his bed and supports his face in his hands. How did he end up here? He looks around him. A narrow room, nice, clean, cold. This entire damn country is cold, what is keeping him here? A souvenir plate on his bedside table, greetings from the *Holstentor*, the Holsten Gate in Luebeck. He mustn't forget to post it to his sister Mary. She keeps every little item he sends her from Germany. Hopefully she will get hold of a parachute badge for him, he has wanted one for a while. Oh fuck, he wasn't going to be defeated by a bit of loneliness. He has been through much worse. But then, however much he tries, there is a void inside him, he cannot fill it.

Interview with Saskia, Germany, 1995

'At some point there I was, working as a waitress in some kind of ice cream parlour - restaurant hybrid. It belonged to a friend of mine, well, friend - acquaintance. It was my first week and I was hoping to get some earning in for the kids. Somehow they had to be fed and I thought maybe there would be leftovers. Food and ice cream seemed a good idea. It was quiet that day, I just stood behind the bar polishing glasses with a towel most of the time.'

Lübeck, Germany, 1968

Grant straightens up and rises to his full height. He opens the wardrobe door, takes out his trench coat and hat, and heads for the door. He needs to get out of here, a bit of fresh air will do him good. Out in the street he realises he has not eaten anything today. Pubs in this country do not close at ten, that's an advantage.

Interview with mother, Germany, 1995

'Suddenly this man walks in. It was like a lightning strike. He was wearing an elegant trench coat with his collar up, like Humphrey Bogart. Anyway, he walked to a table and sat down. The coat was good quality, too, double seams, lovely fabric. He just seemed so familiar to me, as if I had seen him before somewhere. You could tell right away he was English or something, he had a really strong accent, but he was rolling his r's, it was quite sexy. I noticed his lips first, he had very full lips, that is meant to be sensuous. But then, you know that, you have got them, too. I went to get his beer, but when I turned round he was gone. He must have just stood up and left.'

Lübeck, Germany, 1968

That was all he needed. How was he meant to handle that? He could not fall in love now, here in Lübeck of all places, not now he had made up his mind he wanted to return to Dipton. Grant felt something he never felt – pure unadulterated fear. Her face – as if he knew her. These eyes, brown, no green, or brown? There was something sad about them. And suddenly he realises, it is that which connects them.

Interview with Saskia, Germany, 1995

'A quarter of an hour later he returned – with a big bunch of roses. I wasn't even surprised. That's strange, isn't it? The situation seemed familiar somehow.

Lübeck, Germany, 1968

Anna-Ray's father returns to his table. He asks Saskia what she can recommend, and she tells him Schaschlik. Ok then, whatever that was. He could only hope it was not connected to this awful dish Himmel und Hölle - Heaven or hell that the people of this town seemed to love for some inexplicable reason. A few minutes later Saskia brings his plate. Big chunks of grilled meat on wooden skewers, separated with chunks of onion, peppers and tomato, with rice and the obligatory garnish. Looked good, smelled even better, how is he meant to eat it?

Clumsily, he begins to cut the meat from the skewers. 'Oh, please, let me help', she says. A lovely smile, great legs under that dress. She elegantly takes the end of the skewer between thumb and index finger of her slender left hand and begins to push the meat chunks down with a fork in her right hand, no wedding ring. Well, she tries to push it down, but the grill has fused wood and meat together. 'Just a moment, Sir, das haben wir gleich.'

He can see tiny beads of sweat form on her forehead. One more time, with effort now. This time she succeeds, but is surprised by their own strength. The meat not only loosens, it flies across the restaurant, landing with a splash in the bar sink. Saskia stands and looks at the empty wooden stick in her hand. She looks at Grant and they burst out laughing.

Session Twenty-Four

Relax, breathe deeply. Keep breathing. That's good. You are in Germany. It is the 19th of July 1969.

Grant is driving too fast. On the passenger seat his pregnant wife Saskia. She alternates between telling him to slow down and telling him to go faster, depending on the level of her contractions. She doesn't look nine months pregnant, people have been commenting on that. The doctor has told her she has a womb that points to her spine, whatever that means. It's a boy, Grant can feel it. He will not be an Armstrong, the paperwork for his divorce from Gladys has not yet been translated into German. What if something happens to her before they are properly married? Would he have to look after her four children on his own, with a fifth baby to top it all?

Saskia moans, he looks over to her. 'Alles gut?' She nods and waves him to move on. They still communicate mainly with gestures, he has never learned to speak German properly, and she only knows a few English words. Her bump is proof that not all successful communication is verbal. 'Grant, Achtung!' she screams and he can see the oncoming lorry only as a reflection in the corner of his eye. His chest seems to be exploding. He cannot breathe and pains shoot down his left arm. Before his brain has processed the information, his right arm has already turned the steering wheel around. The car swerves, tyres screeching, into the ditch.

The crew of the Apollo 11 pass behind the moon and draw a deep breath as they watch the Sea of Tranquillity.

When Saskia is taken to hospital she is covered in blood. 'It's not my blood' she keeps shouting, but no one listens. 'My children are at home all alone, someone will have to get them! Where's my husband?' she calls out. They don't tell her where Grant is. She delivers a healthy baby girl, ten toes, ten fingers, and a small button nose.

After the baby has been washed and weighed, she is taken away to the nursery, already fast asleep. A young doctor enters and checks Saskia's chart. 'You are Miss Puschat?' 'Yes' She can see from the expression on his face that something is wrong. 'Is the baby ok? Has something happened?' He straightens up. 'Oh no don't worry, it's not about the baby at all. Congratulations by the way and well done!' He pauses, she feels like punching him. Tell me, goddamn you, tell me. I know you enjoy knowing something I don't, you probably get off on the power you prat, but if you don't tell me right now I swear to god, I will.. She stays silent but the doctor catches that glow in her eyes and takes a step back before he says 'I am very sorry, but your ...erm... partner suffered a cardiovascular incident, that means he has had a heart attack.' He gives her a moment but the news is not sinking in. 'Is he...?' 'He is recovering at the moment, but he needs to stay on the intensive care unit for a while. We have told him about the baby and he is delighted.'

Saskia is stunned. Grant, a heart attack? He is only forty-four. Yes, he hides his receding hairline with an over comb, he had all his teeth replaced and he smokes and drinks far too much, but a heart attack? At this moment her son bursts in. 'Mama, are you okay? They picked us up in an ambulance, it was so cool!' Saskia winces slightly as her son throws himself into her arms. She is surprised that her children are allowed in here. They are accompanied by a nurse. 'We thought we'd make an exception. After all, they have big news, haven't they?' 'Big news? You mean about the heart attack?' Her son rolls off the bed quickly and lands on the floor. Her daughters have come in as well, her oldest is holding the baby. 'Have they told you, Mama? Isn't it cool?' Saskia is confused. How can that be cool, it's awful! 'But five thousand Deutschmarks!' her daughter proclaims. Now she really doesn't know what to think. Money? What money? 'Don't look so shocked, Mama, it's great. We've won the lottery!'

Session Twenty-Five

Deep breath, this next bit is not going to be easy. But you can do this, you can always stop, take a breath and continue when you are ready. If it gets too much, look to the top right corner of your eyes, then the top left corner, then the middle. There. Now direct your mind to Durham. On May 30th, 1973, Mary receives a telegram, written in Saskia's indecipherable English. It's a Wednesday.

"GRANT HAS BEEN DEAT BY MAY 23 IN MONDAY JUNE 4 AT 12 P.M. ARE HIS HUMILIATION SASKIA"

He had managed five years with his new wife, her four kids and his own baby daughter. Five years in which he tried hard to convince himself and others that he had not been affected by the war. No one knew about post traumatic stress in those days. To the untrained eye he was simply drinking too much and dreaming badly. He had managed to hold down a job, had managed to not break any of the kids' necks when they silently approached him from behind. He had escaped two heart attacks. The third one got him.

There is a picture of Anna-Ray, she is smiling. She wears a yellow and red dress with a large red strawberry on her chest. She is snuggled up to her aunt Mary, who has come from England with her son. Anna-Ray looks happy. This picture is taken on the day of her father's funeral.

Weeks later her sister finds a bar of chocolate under Anna-Ray's pillow. It has melted a little and lost its shape inside the wrapper. When she tries to persuade her baby sister to throw it away, Anna-Ray refuses, arms crossed. 'I am keeping it for dad, for when he comes back.' The chocolate is still under her pillow when her 18 year old brother comes into her room later that night.

Session Twenty-Six

I want you to break the rules now. I need you to check up on Anna-Ray, and for this reason I need you to read her diary. I know this is not something you would normally do, but she is not doing well. I can tell because her eyes, normally hazel brown, are light green from crying, and she wears far too much makeup. Something happened. She is nineteen years old, in her final year at school, completing her German Abitur, her Leaving Exams.

2 June 1989

My step dad died. That's how fast that goes. He was fooling around in the morning, by the evening he was dead. His sons are devastated, my mum couldn't stop screaming. I didn't know what to do, I held her like a baby and sang lullabies until the doctor came and gave her something. What happens when she wakes up?

The second partner of my mother who simply dies, bang, dead. We all thought, surely not again, surely he is going to be alright, we are all just overreacting because of my dad. But then my brother-in-law called from the hospital, and we just sat in silence for a long time, in one group, all connected.

There is an IRA killer squad in Germany at the moment, they target British military and their families. In Hanover they shot a squaddy, his wife and even his small baby straight in the face with a sawn-off shotgun, through the car windows in a car park. Close to there they shot another squaddie's wife. They apologised when they found out she was German. What goes on in their heads? Jewish, Arian, Irish, Brit, German, where is the difference? Is it starting again? I have to kneel and check for Semtex under the car before I can drive it. What would happen if my boyfriend had an accident? They say they might send them to the Gulf. What will be left of him then? I want a child.

Love Anna-Ray x

Well done. Now let's go deeper. Further back.

9 January 1989, 19 years old

I am going out with a squaddie. Not a great decision and today someone called me a 'Nato mattress'. The English girlfriends don't like me either, they think I am stuck up because I am quiet a lot – but it's just because my English is not good enough to understand them. I know I am doing English Literature at school, but they're not exactly speaking Shakespearean. He means a lot to me, that makes it harder, actually. If he meant nothing, I could easily leave him, but this way I am just tying myself down. He is a soldier (musician, saxophonist) with the British Army, he has English and Italian nationality. We would get our own flat from the army if we were married. My own place – finally! But marriage – fuck that. I don't know anymore. No quiero que te vayas, dolor, ultima forma de amar.

Love Anna-Ray x

That's right, breathe. And now go deeper, further back in time.

25 October 1985, 16 years old

Hi, how are you? I feel semi-shit. Autumn depression, you understand. You do? Funny, I don't.

I actually just wanted to tell you that I am not a virgin anymore. Ok then, let's be open about this, let's give those nosy rummaging police officers something to really want to read.

I didn't have an orgasm, but it hurt like hell. There were still a lot of scars I think, you know from where. He just kept poking around and almost gave up but then it kind of cracked, there was so much blood. He came twice. I don't get this. I should be happy. I said I don't want to do it for a while. The smallest thing and I feel really low, not just physically. I hope he doesn't notice too much. Oh shit, I don't feel like writing anymore.

Love Anna-Ray x

10 October 1985, 16 years old

Ok, it's October 10th and I went to see the gynaecologist this morning. She put me on the pill. After all the horror stories I had heard about these appointments, I hardly noticed, it was over after two minutes. She noticed about the scars though and she asked a few questions but I made excuses. So now I am on the anti-baby pill, I have to say, dentist is worse.

It's high time as well because I spent the night at his house last week and had my first petting experiences. His twin brother shares his bedroom. It was really dark and I quite liked it, but then I noticed there were more than two hands on my body. I pretended I didn't notice.

Love Anna-Ray x

And now further and further back in time.

22 September 1985, 16 years old

Hi, just read my old diary entries – wow, I am glad nobody reads them! I was such a stupid little girl! So much trash, always in love with a different boy, oh God!

But anyway, let's get to the main subject: My boyfriend H, the 21 year old twin. But maybe it's best if I start from the beginning:

On September 6th there was this street festival. I felt like going for it but I swear I really didn't want to meet anyone. Oh well, as things go, I passed one of those All-round bands from Hanover, I saw him, I looked straight at him, he looked back and it was a bit like a staring contest. He was playing the clarinet and I made him laugh so he played a wrong note. I hid for a while after that to make him nervous. When I 'coincidentally' passed him again at 11pm he was so glad to see me again he immediately asked me out. His twin came along as well and both of them tried it on something bad!

Anyway, we got talking on the telephone after that and in the end we met in Hanover. The weather was really awful, it was grey and cold and rainy. We met at his house and first thing after he opened the door he kissed me.

I liked it but then I noticed it was his twin brother!

I won't see him for a while but I think I had better go and make an appointment with the gynaecologist. I will need that pill, he is 21, you know. He doesn't need a little girl, he needs a woman.

Keep going, further in time, further back.

31 October 1983, 14 years old

I just got up (excuse my crappy handwriting) and noticed my period has started for the first time. I don't even have tummy cramps, although I get them all the time when swimming, running, dancing – just when I get that thing where you normally have cramps, I don't. Not that I am angry about that. I am hungry now, I will grab breakfast.

Love Anna-Ray x

Can you hear her voice changing? A young girl now, in the midst of puberty. What happened before this?

23 March 1983, 13 years old

Dear Diary

Sorry I haven't written in a while. I am almost in the eighth grade and slowly school is getting much more demanding. I would be surprised if I had to re-sit though. I started piano lessons. I love playing and I am progressing really fast, I can play 'The Little Negro' by Debussy, that is really cute! But Mama keeps reminding me how expensive this is for her and she always wants me to play in front of visitors. But she hates it when I practise because then the neighbours can hear me make mistakes, so I know this won't last.

I have had to change location three times while writing, there is always someone walking in! So now I have ended up at the desk. I've got the small radio here as well. Let's see what's on, cool, it's 'The Club', I love that!

With boys it's still the same old, same old. I have crushes all the time. At the moment it's a boy in my class, Tom. Oh, and I have a guinea pig now, called Jerry. It's an

Albino and he is a bit weird, but I like that. He gets epileptic fits, and I know I shouldn't, but that makes me laugh. He just squeaks and falls over and then he starts twitching. It looks like break dance!

I am totally into cosmetics, steam, face masks, all that toodeldoodel. Oh man, if I ever read this when I am a grown up I bet I'll laugh at that word! I am curious what I will look like. Hopefully not as fat as now. Oh well, fat is maybe exaggerated, but when I sit down I can count three rings!!! I could go on writing forever but then again, maybe not. So tschüss.

Love Anna-Ray x

Well done, you are almost there. Keep going, keep going back further.

10 December 1981, 12 years old

Dear Diary

I have fallen into a hiatus of crazy dimensions. On the one hand Mama says:"Oh, those Dutch, at least they speak their mind!" On the other hand she doesn't even notice that

that's exactly what I am like! When I speak my mind it's called cheek! I always thought I'd remain unbroken but she will soon drive me there! Then I, too, will become a liar, faking agreement and contentment, just thinking her mind. That makes her against me and that makes me so sad! I do love my Mama. I am already so sad and broken that I am almost hysterical. I can't tell Mama though, she will only misunderstand.

   Love Anna-Ray x

21 September 1979, 10 years old

Dear Diary,

I thought it had finished. A week ago, it happened. The police came and picked him up. They said this time he will be committed, whether Mama tries to stop it or not. She did try, but the judge took guardianship and had him assessed. I think he attacked his psychiatrist or something. They said he is schizophrenic and a risk.

No shit! They still didn't know what he did to me. I didn't care. He was gone, locked up and wouldn't come back. And then there he was. I walked into the kitchen and he was standing behind the door. He had run away. Just walked out with the other visitors of the high security ward, hugged another patient and walked out. Must have looked alright to the guards. He is back in there now, but I know he will be back. He told me so. This will never end. I will never be alright.

Anna-Ray x

Take one more step, just a little further back still.

12 August 1979, 10 years old

Dear Diary

Mama found my diary and she read it! She found the pages where I wrote that I want to kill myself and that no one understands me – and she tore them out and threw them away. She said "What will people think. Just imagine if you get hit by a bus and the police search the house and find your diary. They'll think you killed yourself." How loud do I have to scream before she hears me – she would probably only tell me to shush before the neighbours complain.

I am stunned, paralyzed, my lungs hurt.

Love Anna-Ray x

Session Twenty-Seven

It's time. Focus, take another deep breath in. Focus and you can see Anna-Ray. She is ten.

This is her schedule. Mondays to Fridays 7.55 to 13.10 school. 13.30 to 17.00 library. 17.00 until dark, inside the playhouse on the playground. If lucky, at a friend's house. Weekends in the public swimming pools, Sundays inside churches, any church.

The remainder of the time under tables, inside her wardrobe, under her bed. Reading.

A book on atoms had explained it perfectly. A body is made of cells, the cells are made of atoms. There are only a limited number of atoms in the world. Just like the bricks in a box of Lego, people are built with these atoms. If they die, the atoms let go again and new people are formed, using the same building blocks.

Anna-Ray is fascinated by the fact that every single person on this earth carries multiple atoms of every single other person who died more than 50 years ago. She contains atoms of Rembrandt, Shakespeare, Goethe. Atoms of Tsar Nicholas II were reunited with those of his murdered family. At the same time they have to share her body with parts of their assassins. In a few years, microscopic remains of Holocaust victims would need to bond with atoms of Hitler and his henchmen. No wonder then that she was gradually coming apart at the seams.

A push, a blow and she can no longer feel her body. Her mind lets go, it floats to the ceiling like a Helium balloon. She can no longer smell musty floor tiles, cannot not see the fluorescent lights.

Ten years old now. Too young to move out, but soon, she will soon be too tall to hide under the bed. In the afternoons she is safe. The library has provided her with an endless amount of hideouts. All she has to do is open a book and crawl inside. It takes one or two pages to draw her in completely. She disappears in stages, becomes unresponsive, deaf, mute, loses her sense of time. Then she is granted access, immerses herself fully, for hours and hours, until the warm womb of her refuge spits her out again, leaving her dazed and exposed. Closing time.

She prefers classics, books by authors that died more than fifty years ago, she is connected to them by the breadcrumb trail of tiny atoms they have left all over her body.

Session Twenty-Eight

You are floating further back in time, to Stade, Germany, March 1975.

Anna-Ray has survived seven hundred and thirty days since her fourth birthday. She will finally be able to break loose, she will leave the house with her sisters at seven in the morning and return after school around three, when all the others had come back as well.

She has practised reading since she was four, was able to calculate and name the major countries of the globe. She is fluent in German and understands Dutch and English. She has left nothing to chance, there was no way she was not going to be accepted into the first class at primary school.

When her mum presents her to the headmaster, Anna-Ray detects a frown on the old man's face. She flinches when he approaches her with his arm stretched out, then she notices he is offering to shake her hand. There is a noise in the classroom that worries her, a knocking noise, maybe they have mice? It takes her a while before she realises it comes from her teeth. The chattering seems to spread and take hold of her entire body. He asks for her name and she answers, but her voice stumbles over the lump in her throat and he has to ask her to repeat herself three times before he is satisfied with her reply.

She manages to draw a sketch of herself, walk along a thin line and performs other tasks she has not prepared for. He does not ask for multiplication or literacy skills. When he looks her up and down she becomes aware of how tiny she is for her age. How thin and pale, despite her mother's attempts to rub blusher onto her cheek bones. 'You could be such a pretty child, if only you ate better' she used to say. 'A bit of colour will soon take care of that or else people will think I am not looking after you properly.'

'She will have to carry quite a heavy school bag'. the headmaster says, 'I am not sure she is strong enough to do that quite yet. I think we should maybe wait a year or so until she has matured a bit more.' Ice cold panic rises from

Anna-Ray's stomach, freezing the muscles around her rib cage. She wants to shout out 'No, I am strong enough, I can do this, I can carry anything you want', but her lungs will not surrender enough air to produce a sound. She has been sentenced to a further 365 days of being taken care of by her brother. This time she will eat.

Session Twenty-Nine

You float back further, and further in time.

At five years old Anna-Ray begins to fade away. The scales in her bathroom reassure her she has mass, although 15kg and 104cm prove such weak allies to gravity that she is only barely kept from drifting away. It is a hard enough task to keep her body attached to her mind. When she follows HIM down the steps to the games room, she is sure not all of her follows the entire way down, some of her remains on the steps, like a residue, breadcrumbs to find her way back up when he has finished.

The games room had been her mum's idea. A large cellar room, carpeted with squares of felt intended to provide cosiness but which instead trapped the musty damp basement scent. A bed for sleepovers, skittles, even a ping pong table. A room for fun. A room for happy children. A room where all five of Saskia's kids could have what she never had – a childhood.

A bed. Carpeting to soundproof the room. No windows. Small plastic skittles with razor sharp seams where the two halves were forced together. Pushed inside a small girl's anus, those sharp edges would leave a fine cut, enough to draw blood, but only a few drops, no permanent marks. There was lots of fun to be had.

When they had moved into this house, the children had explored every space excitedly. It was still in the first few days when Anna-Ray's brother showed everyone else the cat. It seemed, he said, the previous tenants had left them a little present, like a voodoo charm. Sick people, he said, shaking his head with a sad expression. Then he winked at Anna-Ray, who was very quiet. The cat was hanging from the low ceiling in the cellar, a small piece of wax sheathed washing line wrapped tightly around her neck. Apparently she had had enough room to put up a fight. She must have hung there for days, struggling, shrieking, slowly growing weaker. It was hard to say whether she had suffocated or starved to death, in any case, no one had heard a sound. And even if someone, maybe a passing neighbour, had heard the sounds, would they have been able to imagine what happened here? Now the weight of her body and decay were pulling her body away from her head. Anna-Ray understood the message loud and clear.

Above ground there are plenty of hiding spaces. Under the table, in her wardrobe, behind the couch. When Anna-Ray sits very quietly, she begins to lose substance almost instantly. She feels every atom in her body push the others away, there is no glue between them, no attachment to hold them together. She is losing density.

Session Thirty

Don't give up now, you are almost there. Deep breaths, just a little further now.

By the time she reaches four, Anna-Ray has the ability to freak out anyone who looks straight at her. It is in her eyes. She tends to stare at you, silently, through the transparent jelly of your eyeballs, scraping past your nerves straight into the centre of your brainstem. Her own eyes are windows, betraying a knowledge that makes you sick to the pit of your stomach. She knows what it is like to scan the room for exits. How to be trapped, on her own, with the monster not under her bed but waiting outside, hammering against the door, screaming for her to let him in or else. She knows how to visualise escape routes, how to weigh up whether breaking her legs jumping out of the window would hurt more than staying. How quickly could her brother run downstairs, how would she escape him with her bones shattered?

Faster knocks, louder, matching her heartbeat. Of course she will eventually have to open the door for HIM. There was no way out, HE would get her anyway. The longer she waits the harder the punishment, she knows the rules. She also knows that her sister will come home from school at thirty five past two. Ghost hour is over then and the monsters return to their graves. It is a tight rope walk between delaying him and keeping the level of his anger to a minimum.

There is no other way. One day, she finds a large spider on the sofa. Her mother has fetched a bottle of insecticide and Anna-Ray watches with interest how the spider's movements slow, how its body curls up and eventually stops twitching. After this she hides the bottle under her bed. Her mother buys a new one. She hides that one as well. Finally, when her brother is sleeping she sneaks into his room, empties the entire bottle and closes the door. She stuffs dish cloths and toilet paper into the crack under his door and returns to bed, sleeping dreamlessly for the first time in months. It will finally be over now. He will never touch her or her sisters ever again. He will never again take out the frying pan against her mum, he will never again hang her sister head down over the rails of the balcony, announcing to the world that he is about to let go of her ankle and watch her brains splatter over the concrete slabs below. What a lot of fun that would have been, he had claimed, disappointed he never got to see what pattern it made, when the cops had guided him to their car. She didn't know the Rorschach rules, if he had discovered a giant beetle in the stain, would some psychiatrist finally have committed him? He will never again ejaculate into her waste basket, never again press his naked stinking body against her sleeping face.

But he does wake up, never even complains of a headache. HE cannot not be killed. It becomes clear to her then that she will have to grow up, survive for as long as possible, until she is big enough to fight him. She needs help, not her neighbours, not the baker, none of the neighbours' kids, no one listens to what she tells them. She needs an army. An army of adult men who love her. She is tough, despite appearances. Her legs like matchsticks, her face malnourished and white. She cannot eat. It is not the chewing, simply the fact that everything she swallows tastes of cum. She has heard that sperm was alive, that the tiny tadpoles can bore their way into the shell of an egg and grow to the size of a baby. When they are in her throat, in her stomach, are they wriggling their way through her windpipe, like maggots? Are they filling her up, filling that empty space the he leaves when he spreads her legs and wraps them around his neck, sucking her soul out through her vagina?

The plaster next to the door is beginning to crumble. A crack has appeared, running all the way parallel to the left side of the door frame. It widens every time his fist beats the wood. "Who knows who is really mad?" the psychiatrist had said when the family had gone to support Schorsch's therapy. "We may think it is Schorsch, but is that not a matter of perspective? We label him schizophrenic but what does that actually mean?" No one had heard the scream in her head, a deep guttural scream, the scream of a trapped and anxious cow just before her throat is cut and she is transformed into a lump of meat.

Silence now. Fifteen minutes to two. His gentle voice worms its way through the wood. "If you come out now I promise I won't hurt you. I love you, you know that. What we are doing is not bad, you know. There are lots of examples in history where this is normal. Lots of stories have been written about brothers and sisters that love each other." Yes, I know, it is a matter of perspective, a matter of time and place, of strength and endurance. A matter of knowing that she will pass out when this grown man's hand covers her mouth and nose, when his wrist rests on her throat, when he presses harder and harder, supporting his entire body weight on this hand to free the other. It's a matter of perspective if she is lucky to wake up again. Afterwards it will be important to be polite, not to make him think that she might tell on him. She knows to him she is nothing but evidence, something he will eventually get rid of.

She knows because a few weeks back she woke up inside a tiny dark box. When she climbed out, she could see that she had been lying in an old lead ammunitions box. They had found that in the cellar as well, a remnant of the war perhaps. The box was outside in the garden, a shovel was lying next to it. Maybe she had been unconscious longer than usual. Maybe he thought he had killed her. Maybe it was more thrilling to know she would wake up underground.

She knows she can delay him no longer. Afterwards she will ask if she can please put her jeans back on. The ones with the little plastic bugs for buttons. Yellow plastic ladybirds.   She   turns   the   key.

Session Thirty-One

I know you want to leave this scene, so let's give you a break. Look up to the top right corner, then to the top left corner, then to the middle. Deep breath. Focus on the gathering, the funeral scene in the Scottish Borders. It is right NOW.

Even before the solicitor takes out a piece of white paper from his top pocket and reads the message she has left them, the crowd of men have begun to suspect their purpose at this ceremony. Her husband is the first to truly understand. He had told her millions of times how much he wished she could see herself through his eyes. Whenever she had lost hope and began to doubt herself he wished she could see how much he loved and believed her. Every time he had been with her he had felt her flinch. Every time he had shouted at her he had felt how afraid she was, how she had withdrawn into a corner of the room. He had hated himself in these moments, and it was this realisation that caused him to turn away from her bed, night after night, knowing she was awake, waiting. It is not her love for them that had drawn them to her, it had been the way she made them feel about themselves. They saw their own reflection in her adoring eyes, and they liked what they saw. To begin with, her love had been unconditional, but then she began to question them, began to withdraw, and the light in her eyes flickered before it extinguished. They all had become rapists to her, had hurt her beyond repair. But all of them knew she was reacting to something much older, something that had taken hold in her chest, attempted to pull her back, while she ran as fast as she could, never catching up with her racing thoughts.

Each one of them had replaced a memory, had repaired some small part of her. They were symptoms of the abuse. They were the cure. Their cocks had been the knitting needles required to abort her trauma, their sperm had flushed out her womb and collaborated in an act of creation.

They might have stroked her in a way she needed to be stroked or kissed her where she needed to be kissed, might have given her an image of herself that she had never seen before, that she could add to her repertoire of fragmented identities. They had given her thoughts and memories to dislodge those that were eating her inside out.

They have given her boundaries, have taught her what she didn't want, what she wasn't prepared to accept. They have been a sounding board to her rage, the pain of iodine poured onto an open wound. She has seen her own reflection in them, has built a construct of herself with the building blocks they had handed her. Now they are all here, mere reflections of the constructs she has built of them. Their thoughts are no longer their own, these are hers, narcissistic projections of how they might act if placed in this situation. They have all moved on, found new lives, new women to hold on to. They have all aged, some have died. But these men are frozen in her love for them, distorted by the prism of her gratitude for the pieces they have returned to her.

The solicitor, now dressed in full court robes, adjusts his white wig and begins to state her case:

'Merriam-Webster's Dictionary of Law defines **recovery** as *1 : the act, process, or fact of recovering 2 a : the obtaining, getting back, or vindication of a right or property by judgment or decree; especially : the obtaining of damages*

When has a person recovered? What has been recovered? Empowerment? Hope? Is recovery not more of an absence of symptoms? How would one exterminate such symptoms? And if the symptoms to be exterminated have been completely absorbed by the applicant then who would pass such a decree? Who would execute the judgement?

Who has a right to exist? Murder need not be a crime of passion. It can be a crime of compassion. This is not a place of retribution, it is a place of reconciliation, of endings nevertheless. The body of a child was wrongfully executed, no public spectacle was ever made of this. You, gentlemen, have resuscitated the corpse. You are the enforcers, exempt from liability but not allegiance. You were a part of her so long, she has loved and hated every single one of you, and now she will claim back what she has invested. Damages must be obtained. This crime will be on her conscience alone, not on yours.'

'What does he mean? What crime?' Excitement in the group increases markedly. The rain is falling now, heavy drops that wash away the neat boundary around the freshly dug hole.

'She obviously wants us to do something. I don't think we are here to bury her.' 'How do you mean, just check the coffin, there she is, what else are we meant to do, do you think?'

The professor, being a man of science, is naturally the first to lunge towards the coffin. The lid has been tied down with simple canvas straps and it does not take him long to undo the loose bows. No one questions him. The others seem distracted by the creature in the grave. It is attempting to climb out, reaching for roots, stones, anything to give him a solid hold in the wet soil. But the ground is too soft, again and again he slides back inside the hole.

When Günther throws open the lid, he gasps.

Session Thirty-Two

One more time, just this once, I need you to go back. You are in Germany again, a few months after Anna-Ray's father has died.

'I am glad you have come to your senses.' Schorsch towers over her, smiling. He is nineteen years old. His head is shaven, his eyebrows missing. His smile reveals a row of perfectly even teeth. His canines are sharp, stained by his compulsion to smoke anything he can get his hands on - rolled up newspapers and cinnamon sticks if there was nothing else. She knows his teeth, they have left marks on her skin. She bruises easily, even then. Her mum calls her clumsy. Everyone knows she is odd. They laugh about the way she hides under the table when visitors come and feel embarrassed about the way she clings on to some of them. Especially the male ones. She loves her Dutch uncle Leo desperately and begs him to take her with him when he leaves. Cute.

Schorsch kneels down in front of her now. He wraps his arms around her, both stiffen. He can smell her fear. "Come, I have a present for you", he whispers, nibbling her earlobe. Rising to his full size he takes her hand into his. The tips of his fingers are stained brown, too. Nicotine, cinnamon, whatever. Her nails are chewed down to the flesh. She can smell the grill warming up inside the oven. Is he making dinner for them?

'You have to see it from my perspective', he purrs. 'You need to make a choice now. It can only be one or the other. But at least you get a choice. I guess you are lucky that way.'

Schorsch points at the table. There is a pair of brand new roller skates. Disco rollers, four thick rubber wheels attached to trendy sneakers, still packaged. Girl's skates, small enough for a clumsy girl with match stick legs. Schorsch lightly touches her lips. His fingers taste salty and smell of tobacco.

'It's not as if I want to do this. You are, in fact, leaving me no choice whatsoever. You broke the rule, didn't you?'

The girl nods suspiciously, staring at the skates. This is new. He is angry, she can tell. And yet he is giving her a gift? Or had he planned to give them to her and will now simply take them away?

The smell from the grill is naked, without the usual lure of cooked meat. She notices a slight note of burned cleaning liquid, her mother must have cleaned the cooker the day before. Little beads of sweat form on her forehead.

'It's getting hot in here, isn't it?' His face moves closer to hers. She closes her eyes and can feel his rough tongue licking over her skin, lapping up every drop.

'That's better, isn't it?' he coos.

The next few seconds pass in an instant. He grabs hold of her wrist and drags her towards the oven. She can see the yellow glow of

the grill pipes, winding their way along the ceiling of the oven, before he presses her wrist against the red hot metal. The smell of burned flesh, mixed with burned hair, a sizzling noise as the pipe digs its way towards her bone. Not far past midday. Plenty of time yet.

Session Thirty-Three

I feel you are ready now. So come back to our gathering in Scotland. Help us finish this.

There is no body inside the wicker coffin. Instead, it is filled with books – some leather bound, some simple note pads. Some are pink and girlie, some brown and professional. Günther realises he has opened the lid in such a way that it is blocking the view to the others. 'It's books!' he shouts. 'Just books!' Lothar joins him, followed by Ferdinand. They reach inside the coffin and start leafing through the pages. Behind them, the creature in the grave is still toiling to free himself.

'They are diaries', Ferdinand exclaims, 'There must be over a hundred of them. This is her entire life!'

He picks up a small pink one and notices that the lock has been cut open. The first page is titled 'My brother', so is the second and the third. There are stories about her love affairs, "my army of lovers" as she calls them. There are stories about her father, her mother, about the clan that she belongs to. All of them are written in a surprisingly naïve style, like a romance novel. But every one of them is titled 'my brother'. He does not bother checking the rest of the books. He needs no further hints.

The other two are leafing through similar pages, her life has been a singular attempt to burn her candle at both ends, but her brother had taken the oxygen out of the equation. She had summoned them to help her live, not die.

She had been raised on stories of her father's life, all a little too heroic to ring entirely true. They all know them, she has recited them often enough. In the end it had been her Armstrong roots that had brought her back to this country, her father's country. His stories had all been about survival, INVICTUS MANEO. They had given her strength. What she hadn't learned from family members she had pieced together from letters, museum visits, and Internet research. Bit by bit he had become a person, he was no longer missing. A little idealised maybe, but a strong role model for her to follow, someone to look after her.

It was only when she began to research her father that she had begun to realise she had learned much of her strength from her mother. But while her father's stories were adventurous, lengthy and detailed, told by those he had left behind, those who did not want to tarnish his memory, her mother had not been so forthcoming. Her life became a hurried account of censored details. Strung together like the pearls on a necklace, one only wore on special occasions. She revealed only those facts she wanted her daughter to know, vacuums remained unfulfilled. Why verbalise what could not be explained, why her mother chose a violent paranoid schizophrenic as her babysitter – a man who was bursting with hormones and yet could not find a girlfriend to accept him – why she gave him full access to a little girl who was already traumatised by her father's death. Why she covered this up for years and told Anna-Ray to remain silent. Both her and her mother were stunned by this, and their relationship calcified into the cast of someone else's mother-daughter sculpture.

The men look at each other. 'We know what we have come to do' they tell Anna-Ray's advocate. The solicitor nods. Reluctantly at first, then with more and more determination, the men gather around the grave in a circle, clutching their shovels and pick axes. It does not matter now who has seen the content of the diaries, it no longer matters why they are all here, different ages, alive when they should be dead. They are constructs. Her constructs. She has built herself an army. Now it is up to them to deconstruct the script she has acted to for so many years. Time has no relevance here, it is neither linear nor logical.

The creature gains hold of a tree root sticking out at the side of the grave. He pulls himself up, heaving his upper body beyond the soggy earth, which lines the top of the hole. He manages to pull his legs up under his belly and falls forward into a crouch, like a feral cat about to jump on its prey. They all stand and watch, long enough to recognise his astonished face, feeling the rush in their ears, the tension in their jaw muscles, before the first of them lunges forward and grabs hold of Anna-Ray's brother. The frenzy begins.

They tug and hack, tear his clothes away and bury their hands deep in his guts before he has time to comprehend what is happening. Pick axes are raised and aimed carefully, severing his limbs one by one, exposing bone fragments until he is nothing but lumps of flesh, goulash.

They pause, pleased with a job well done, then one by one they jump into the grave, taking the pieces with them.

Session Thirty-Four

Hamburg   29 May 1998

The bath water has now become completely cold and Anna-Ray's body has begun to fight back with shivers, goose bumps, withdrawing its arteries from the surface into deeper, warmer tissue.

She has read somewhere that the human body renews itself every seven years. Every atom in her body will continually move, until it has finally moved on, replaced by another. She will not be herself anymore. By the time the next transformation cycle is complete, she will have a brand-new, thirty-six year old body.

A knock on the door startles her. 'Mum, I need a pee! I am bursting!' She smiles, rises from the cold water and wraps her body in a fresh white towel. 'Coming, honey.'

Session Thirty-Five

No, you don't have to imagine this anymore. You can keep your eyes wide open now, one – two – three – you are fully back in the room. What is happening now is real.

Hamburg   August 1998

It was a beautiful day. Hamburg was bathed in the typical dry warmth of a European summer. You remember feeling astonished at how large the apartment was, now that it stood empty. Tiny specks of dust hovered on sunrays. Despite the efforts of an industrial strength Rug Doctor carpet cleaning machine, little dark marks on the pigeon blue floor told of your son drawing over the lines. You were glad that you had been unable to erase all evidence of your existence here. You have spent the last two months functioning, an android, taking one step at a time, breathing in, two, three, hold, out, two, three, four, hold. Your rib cage felt as if it was made of brittle sticks, barely able to contain the flimsy bag of your heart muscle, fluttering away in the squall of your thoughts. Fight or flight was the only system still firing on all cylinders. Your emotions had absconded, like a sulking child they were crouching in some dark fissure of your being, aching to be found. You weren't looking.

You had decided to sell all your furniture, the king-size four poster, the dark blue chaise longue, your beloved wicker chairs, even the shelves. You smiled when you looked at the rawlplugs peaking out from holes in the walls, evidence that you had hoped to settle this time, enough to buy permanent fixtures. Your mum had been outraged when you had installed the climbing frame for your son. 'In the living room? Is that necessary? Why don't you let him play in his own room that would leave the living room for visitors.' 'Mum, my son is more important than visitors, and I quite like having him around me, I don't want to shove him into his bedroom.' It was true, you thoroughly enjoyed being in the proximity of your child. His little body was brimming with life, every cell in his skin capable of sensory pleasure: from the rich milky smell long ago of a baby falling asleep during nursing, one corner of his mouth twitching like the flicker of a satisfied grin, the glow of absolute bliss after smearing an entire pot of yoghurt over his face and arms, the joy of feeding tiny blobs of ice cream to this astonished boy for the very first time, and recently, the joy at spending time with you, his mother, building a pirate ship made of Lego bricks. He was only seven; your mother would have expected him to look after himself at that age – or passed the responsibility on to someone even less suitable. Although your mother lived on a North Sea island near the beach, you hardly visited her. Saskia rented out part of her home to holiday guests. Whenever you visited, it was expected that the child would neither be seen nor heard, kept a secret that you were determined to expose.

(You don't know this yet, but your mother will find a peculiar end. She will never understand what she did to you, will never take responsibility. But she will be loving towards you and will support you in any way possible. She will open her house to you and your future children. When she is ninety years old, she will celebrate in style. All her grandchildren, great-grandchildren, you and your siblings will be invited. She will have passed on an enormous amount of knowledge to all of them, and her genes have ensured that her rebellious streak, her fiery curls and her sharp intelligence will be available to all of you, albeit in a dormant state. She will wait until the guests have left and then walk to the fishmongers, where she will purchase no less than twenty-seven smoked eels. She will hire a motorboat, and, surprisingly sprightly for her age, she will venture out into the open sea. When the petrol runs out she will eat every single one of the eels, until there are none left. Without hesitation, she will roll herself over the side of the boat and sink into the ocean. I am telling you this now, because you will never find out what happened to her.)

You had posted your personal belongings to the new address in the Borders of Scotland. Twenty-five neatly packed boxes full of books, mixed with clothes to keep the weight in each box under thirty kilograms. Sixty Deutschmarks postage each, back to the roots for one thousand five hundred Marks. You had found the cottage when you travelled to Langholm for the annual gather of your clan. As one of the directors of the board of the Clan Armstrong charity you made this journey twice a year. The clan had been a source of strength to you, knowing that you had roots somewhere, knowing that you came from a clan of survivors. Invictus Maneo – I remain unvanquished. It did not matter to you that the clan consisted mainly of elderly members researching genealogy (although you never saw the point, after all, your ancestors were all cattle thieves, weren't they?). It was the motto that got you through much of the last few months, while your cheeks were stitched from the inside, when your face was so swollen you had to tell the radio station you would not return to work. In the end you had decided against going to the police. You had been in the middle of a custody battle with Ferdinand – how would this reflect on your claim that you were the psychologically more stable parent? With the perpetrator still on the loose, with a judge who had to fulfil his quota of granting custody to fathers in order to maintain his reputation as a modern and open minded professional, you had seen only one option. Fuck fight. Flee! You looked around once more – better get downstairs, where your son was already waiting in your friend's car, excited to be going on the big ferry. You spotted the tool case, which was still lying on the floor, it would come in handy when you had to rebuild your life in that abandoned cottage. You picked it up and stuffed it into your handbag; then you locked the armoured front door behind you.

Session Thirty-Six

You leave all this behind. You travel back to your parents, to Saskia and Grant in July 1969. The nurse has rolled your dad into your mother's hospital room. He is still weak from his heart attack but released from the ICU. While your umbilical cord was being cut, his body was wired up to machines. Now you are both disconnected and free to go. The nurse lifts your newborn body out of the glass cot and places you in Grant's outstretched arms. You look fragile against the massive frame of this man. Saskia reminds him to watch your head. He adjusts your tiny body against his, and makes a quiet promise. 'I will look after you, sweet pea. Nothing, nothing whatsoever will ever happen to you, I swear. Your mummy and I will protect you. From now on, it will be all unicorns, rainbows and fluffy bunnies for you, my girl.' And he places a gentle kiss on your forehead while you look up at him.

Ok, maybe this did not happen. And then again, maybe it did.

The End